Other books by Ted Wojtasik:

No Strange Fire

COLLAGE

a novel

Ted Wojtasik

Livingston Press
at
The University of West Alabama

copyright © 2004 Ted Wojtasik
All rights reserved, including electronic text
ISBN 1-931982-33-3 library binding
ISBN 1-931982-34-1, trade paper

Library of Congress Control Number 2003114284

Printed on acid-free paper.

Printed in the United States of America, Livingston, AL

Hardcover binding by: Heckman Bindery

Typesetting and page layout: Gina Montarsi
Proofreading: Gerald Jones, Gina Montarsi,
Derrick Conner, and Joe Taylor

Cover design:Gina Montarsi
Cover art: letters from creative writing class;
photo montage by the author & Gina Montarsi

I would like to
thank my editor, Joe Taylor, and the entire staff at Livingston
Press for their professionalism, efficiency, off-beat tact, eye for detail,
and courage in publishing this novel that I thought might never get
published. Once again, thank you.

Livingston Press is part of The University of West Alabama,
and thereby has non-profit status.
Donations are tax-deductible:
brothers and sisters, we need 'em.

first edition
6 5 4 3 3 2 1

Dedicated to the Memory of

Rhea Johnson
Katherine Anne Porter
Glenway Wescott
&
especially
Monroe Wheeler

What do you say to a young man dying?

The name starts the visibility.

                           Zeljko Matejcic.

Zee, for short—pronounced just like

        The name is Yugoslavian.

                   the last letter in the American

That night, after work,

alphabet. I rode the Metro from downtown Washington to the
National Institute of Health in Bethesda, Maryland, to see

                  Matthew.

In the hall I saw Nurse Scott   frowning at a chart on a clipboard.

I called her name and abruptly she looked up and over.

When she saw me, her face discomposed, her eyes tilting into
sorrow.

"When?" I asked.

"This morning, Zee. At ten o'clock."

The same time Commander Robert Edwin Peary, Jr. stood for
the first time on

"I'm sorry, Zee."

        the North Pole.

I stood there on the third floor. In the hall.   Not moving.

Dr. Thornton stepped out of a room and walked over to me.

"Mr. Matejcic, may I have a word with you in my office?"

I followed him down a long corridor.

After he talked to me about the test results and explained and counseled and admonished, I asked Nurse Scott if I could see Matthew's room again.

"Could I be alone for a moment, please?"

"Of course, Zee."

She shut the door behind her.

The hospital bed had been stripped.

The chair I sat in yesterday had been pushed to one corner.

In the back wall,

>the window,

>>a wisteria blue square,

>>like a Rothko painting,

>>luminous,

>>>lifted and   floated.

The light from the fading summer sky possessed the room.

I stood at the end of the bed, my hands holding the aluminum railing, and stared at the blue-and-gray lines in the mattress.

What do you say to a young man dying?

I looked down at my hands and tightened my grip.

To die no more.

My hands, my privilege, my consummation.

I climbed into the hospital bed, curled up on my side, and

At the foot of the hospital bed in the Bangor Municipal Hospital in Bangor, Maine, my mother stopped and I stopped beside her. closed my eyes. The top of my head was level with the aluminum rails that fenced in my grandmother.

I took my mother's hand.

At the head of the hospital bed my grandfather, his shoulders drooped and his head bent down, sagged in a chair.   He stared at the linoleum floor.

I shifted my weight from one foot to the other and studied the top of his head. His hair was a mass of Manet gray—thick and shaggy and brushed back off his high forehead, tucked behind his ears. Had I ever seen the top of my grandfather's head before?

I shifted my weight back to the other foot.

My eyes shuffled the white curtains, the white walls, the white blankets, the white sheets—I started to build a snowman. I rolled a colossal ball of snow in the front yard. My eyes blinked and winked in the cold as I set a smaller ball of snow on top of the first one. I touched the tip of my tongue

to the half-finished snowman   to taste the cold.

What is a snowman? Snow   curves   cold   white

Finally my eyes settled on my grandmother's face. Her bright, black, glittering eyes were dim and flat.

My snowman   tumbled.

My grandfather lifted his face and fixed his dry eyes upon us.

In Serbo-Croatian, he whispered, "She is gone."

My mother let out a thin cry and dropped my hand, raising her own hands to her face.

I clutched at the pleats I stared at my grandfather's mouth.

"Gone where, *Djed*?" I asked.   in her wool skirt.

That morning—cold, bleak, windy. "Gone where?"

I thought I was going to die, too, or that I wanted to die. At the cemetery, snow fell fast. Grandfather gone.

I looked from headstone to headstone at the different sizes and shapes and the angels and the marble Christs.

Gone.

When my grandfather died, acres of fields opened up in my chest. He had always petted me, hugged me, rubbed his old, wrinkled face into mine.

I would never feel his face again.

As the men lowered the coffin into the frozen ground, the snow swirled around the marble Christs and against the distant pines. The snow swirled through the black-clad figures of men and women

       gathered to honor

The swirling snow danced around my feet and flew up

and I looked up   at the snow

      vanishing

          my grandfather.

into the cold sky.

A free death is supreme conclusion.

The cold, the snow, the trees.

What is a free death?

Not too early, not too late   —the consummation of a victorious life.

Those left behind billow

The arctic region of the heart.

          with courage, hope, and promise.

I placed my month-old memos in an expandable folder, affixed a blue stick-um dot in the upper right-hand corner to indicate my department, and called the messenger service to pick it up to be filed away.

      Tired and spinning into boredom as I waited to sign the release forms, I cut one of the blue dots   in half with a pair of scissors.

What do you say to a young man dying?

      One half

of the blue dot

fell on a clean sheet of typing paper.

The curve and the sharp blue edge on the white background
pulled my eyes to it.

I pressed my thumb on the half dot to fasten it to the paper, held
it up in front of me.   The position

        and the angle

      of the blue   half

dot

      entranced

        me as remote impressions of Mondrian
and Kandinsky sifted through my mind.

I set the paper down and with a Flair pen drew a blue line
around the blue half dot. I held that up and examined it.

I set it down and drew another short, straight blue line in the
corner opposite the blue-circled blue shape.

        I held that up and studied it.

The blue lines and the blue shape, attached to some buried
sensation I couldn't identify, seemed to float before my eyes—but
that didn't matter.

I wanted to honor the color.

I drew another short, straight blue line opposite the other one.

When I held that up, however, I saw that I had destroyed the
balance.

I crumpled the paper into a ball.

I placed the other half of the blue dot on another sheet of typing
paper and held that up.

                  Too far in the corner.

I crumpled that paper into a ball.

I cut another blue dot in half and placed it on another sheet of paper.

I held that up, studied it, set it down, drew a wiggly blue line.

"Zee?"

I looked up, startled. "Miss Doin."

"What are you doing?"

Crumpled sheets of paper covered my desktop. I had the tip of my pen resting against the curve of a blue dot on a clean sheet of typing paper.

"Doodling."

"Doodling?" she said coldly.

Miss Doin, the Assistant Archivist for the National Archives, stared at the crumpled sheets of typing paper. Her stare was as direct and as intense as she was. In her mid-forties, she had worked and battled her way into this position through four successive administrations, budget cuts, and political manipulations. She actually pursed her lips, painted a bright red, the only make-up she ever wore.

"I guess I got a little carried away," I said.

"I suppose so," she said slowly. "I've been buzzing you on the intercom now for five minutes with no answer. Mr. Wilson, the lawyer representing the Peary family, is here to discuss the transfer of materials from the National Geographic Society. I suggest you clear your desk, so we can discuss the arrangements."

I could hardly concentrate on the conversation, since blue lines and blue shapes and blue circles were skimming across my attention. At points in the discussion, Miss Doin glanced sharply at me to indicate that I was *not* presenting myself in as professional a manner as she expected, given the importance of this material.

"To honor the wishes of the Peary family that all papers of

Commander Peary be located in one central depository," Mr. Wilson explained, "the National Geographic Society is prepared to turn over all its holdings to you. Most of this recent material had been discovered accidentally in unmarked boxes in a storage room." He looked from me to Miss Doin. "If you can imagine. . . . "

"The National Geographic is a rather old and a rather large institution," Miss Doin said.

"That's true, quite true," Mr. Wilson agreed. "Still—unmarked boxes? Cardboard boxes? Over fifty or sixty years old? Amazing. Simply amazing. The National Geographic doesn't even know what the contents are. The Peary family has requested—to avoid any possible controversy—that it be deemed confidential and unavailable for research until a thorough classification has been made and presented to them."

I listened politely, nodding occasionally.

"Given the time to work out all legal matters pertaining to such a transaction, I don't anticipate that the Peary material will be transferred to

What does matter? Balance.   your offices until the fall of this year." To balance one cold ball on top of the other.

To taste the cold.

My eyes are intensely dark—the irises as dark as the pupils.

Commander Robert Edwin Peary, Jr. was 53 years old when he discovered the North Pole on April 6, 1909.

5) Sado-masochism.

My hair is black—a tangled, thick mass of Pollock black swirls.

What is sado-masochism?

At ten o'clock that morning, Peary ground his heel into the top of the world, cast his sharp gaze out over the frozen expanse, and saw only the color white—red white and blue.

My face is lean and high-cheekboned—all Picasso angles.
The friendship between the Marquis de Sade, a French nobleman,
and the Chevalier Leopold von Sacher-Masoch, an Austrian nobleman.

At least I was wearing denim jeans when I walked at midnight
into the Falcon, a leather bar in downtown Washington, D.C. :

       With a straight back I stand at exactly six feet. I have
no hair on my chest.

These two aristocrats chronicled their sex lives   Doesn't everyone have a chronicle of his or her own sex life?

    for posterity.

I have broad shoulders because I swim the butterfly.   My calves
are well-defined and muscular.
sawdust-strewn floors,

All the men inside were dressed in some form of leather, resem-
bling

          cowboys
      black walls,
  or motorcycle gangs
          layers of thick blue smoke,
      or crusaders from the Dark Ages.   dimmed lighting.

A huge black man, obviously the bouncer, with a shaved head
and biceps the size of grapefruits, stood just inside the entrance with
his arms folded over his bare chest. An Hispanic man trudged in
with aviator sunglasses fixed on his narrow nose and a studded collar strapped around his neck.

"Could I have a Budweiser, please?" I asked the bartender, a
man with a florid complexion and oily eyes, wearing a leather beret
fastened on his head like a skullcap. A filterless cigarette drooped
from his dark lips.

He slammed down a bottle of Budweiser on the bartop.

"First time here?" he asked, frowning.

I nodded.

"Be careful, that's all I can tell ya. Just last week, a college type like yerself wandered in here and walked off into one of those back rooms with a guy I never seen here before and had to have a broken beer bottle pulled out of his ass. Not a pretty sight, let me tell ya, blood all over the floor, and we caught hell from the police."

I looked at my bottle of beer.

"Yeah," he said, "and it was a Budweiser, too. King of beers."

"Thanks for the advice."

King of beers.

"Yeah, well, let me give ya a little more advice," he said, pulling the cigarette from his lips and spitting a bit of tobacco on the floor. "If yer in here to look, look, then get outta here. My customers don't appreciate gawkers, ya unnerstand? And if yer gonna do sumthin, do it but be careful, like I tole ya."

"I'll be careful."

"Let me tell ya sumthin else. If yer gonna do sumthin and yer new to this, don't let anyone tie ya up back there. Don't don't don't. Cuz that guy that ties ya up may not untie ya and then those bastards'll be all over ya, ya unnerstand?"

I nodded.

He took a final drag on his cigarette, crushed it out, and moved down the bar to fix a drink.

I turned around on the barstool to look out at the crowd. Two white men, ten-gallon hats perched on their heads, played pool directly in front of me. I looked past them to the dark doorway in the far wall.

"So, are you going to hightail it out of here?"

I turned to my right. "What's that?"

"Are you going to hightail it 'outta here' now?"

The man who spoke to me leaned against the bar, holding a bottle of Budweiser.

"No," I said, "I don't think so."

He had a severe crewcut, a square not unhandsome face, and a handlebar mustache. He had on black leather jeans and cowboy boots. He sipped his beer.

King of

"Al—that's the bartender—tells that broken-bottle story to every college-type kid he sees in here."

beers.

"Did that really happen?"

"Two years ago, not last week."

"Why does he tell it?"

"To scare you off. Most of them just turn around and leave. You see, Al hates guys who come in here to stare at us. We're in here to drink and have a good time and we don't need a bunch of tourists pointing fingers at us. Know what I mean?"

I nodded.

A bare-chested man with a hairy chest and a hairy back and the face of a bulldog strolled past the pool table wearing only a pair of black leather chaps. His hairy ass grinned as it disappeared into that dark doorway.

That dark doorway.

What's back there? Tied up?

What's going on back there as I sit here sipping my beer?

What type of pain inflicted

"So you're not going to hightail off, huh?"

to induce pleasure?

"No, I'm not."

"Well, pretty boy, watch yourself more than you watch us."

And he walked away.

Pretty boy.

Who does he think he is to call me pretty boy?

Watch yourself more than you watch   A philosopher in cowboy boots.   us.   I'll jam this Budweiser bottle right up *your* ass and see how much you

"Don't call me a fucking cunt!" one of the pool players with the ten-gallon hat shouted   wriggle and writhe.

and punched a man straight in the face. The man staggered back into the cigarette machine, dropping his beer bottle. It smashed open

"You fucking cunt!" the man bellowed and jumped on the pool player, knocking him to the floor. on the floor. The ten-gallon hat slid over to my feet.

Onlookers surrounded the two fighting men. The black man with biceps the size of grapefruits pushed his way into the crowd.

I moved away from the fight, farther into the bar, closer to that dark doorway.

A broken beer bottle pulled out of his ass. Don't let anybody tie Pretty boy. ya up.   The skin on my arms prickled, my face twitched, and awkwardness knotted the back of my neck. I shouldn't go in there. I ought to leave.

But then you wouldn't

I took a long sip on my Budweiser and stepped into the dark doorway. know.

I couldn't see at first and stopped until my eyes adjusted to the darkness. I glanced back out the doorway, the outer room thick with drab yellow light and moving bodies. I stood in a dark corridor and saw another doorway, in the distance,

I heard moans and sharp slaps.glowing a somber red.

When I reached the red doorway, it opened into a room the size of   I could smell the sour odor of poppers. A single red bulb dangled from the ceiling.   a dorm room.

Three men, intertwined like a Giacometti sculpture, were fucking on a mattress tossed on the concrete floor. One man, on his hands and knees, was completely naked. Another man, his jeans dropped, stood in front of him and fucked him in the mouth, while another man, wearing only a leather harness and cowboy boots, fucked him in the ass. Two other men stood watching, sipping beers, smoking cigarettes. I stood at a distance. No one said a word. The only sounds were moaning and the slapping of flesh against flesh.

I lit a cigarette and watched.

How the priests would consider this evil—this display of sexual strangers. Three men engaged in pure pursuit of lust with no other end than lust itself. If it does not lead, expand, or emerge into something greater, that is the evil—not the lust in itself. Can this type of behavior ever lead into

There were two other doorways in this small room.

something else?

When I finished my cigarette, I walked through the doorway on the right.

Two men were buttressed against the wall of the corridor. As I passed them, each one reached out to feel my crotch and ass.   I saw another doorway in the distance, this time a murky green.

This room was the size of a small gymnasium. It reeked of pot and sweat. Men were wedged in the corners or clumped around objects in the open.

I stood rigid in a dark corner.

Despite the many men, there was a virtual absence of voices—no one talked. The men responded solely to body communication, sensitized to erotic needs.

In one corner a young man with blond hair was tied up in a leather-and-chain sling suspended from the ceiling. His arms were twisted into the chains with his legs spread wide, his feet tied higher than his hands. A leather strap supported his back. He hung there, stretched out like a human hammock, waist high from the floor. He was dressed in a black tank top and black jeans, but the crotch to his jeans had been ripped open.

A muscled black man dipped his hand into a can of Crisco on the floor, stroked his cock hard, and then started to fuck this blond-haired man. When the black man first entered him, the blond-haired man cried out, "Oh God oh God."

A white man with the face of an ostrich stroked his cock hard with the Crisco. Once the black man finished, that man started to fuck the man in the sling.

"Oh God oh God."

A line formed.

In another corner, a naked man knelt in a small basin-like enclosure while another man pissed in his mouth. Urine dribbled down his chin and neck and chest. A man stood nearby snapping a leather belt.

In the center of the room, a slender black man was tied to a wooden cross. A white man, as fat as a pygmy hippo, holding a rosary in his hand, licked the black man's knees.

As I stood watching, transfixed in this underworld, someone started to rub my crotch. Without looking, I moved a couple of steps to the side, but he followed me and started to rub my crotch

"Oh God oh God."

again.   I dropped my hand down to brush his hand away,
but

        he grabbed my wrist, "Don't say a word or I'll cut you,
wrenched my arm up behind my back,   you understand?"
he said, his lips pressed   into
and slammed me face forward into the wall.   my ear.

        My stomach exploded. I nodded. I whispered, "Wha—"
He twisted my arm up higher.

"Don't talk."

I whimpered. He was tearing my shoulder out of its socket! I
had a sudden whiff of cinnamon. Certs? He licked the side of
From the corner of my eye, I saw a black leather mask.

    my face.

The side of my face and chest were pressed against the wall.
He let my arm down and fumbled with the buttons to my jeans. He
pulled them down to my knees. His hand pushed against the middle
of my back, while his other hand kneaded my rear end. He
crouched down, ripped my underwear apart, and buried his face in
my ass. He spread my cheeks and rimmed me.

    "Oh God oh God."

I closed my eyes and felt a tear tickle my cheek. I stood in the
back room of the Falcon while some strange man   Humiliation and
contempt creased my forehead. Saliva dribbled down my inner
thigh. wearing a black leather mask rimmed me.How he *wanted*
me. But what He stood up. did he want? "Take my finger in your
mouth." He shoved his hand in my face and his middle finger in between my lips. "Suck it, suck it good, get it good and wet."

    Then he stuck that finger straight up my ass. I gasped as he
rammed it in and out.

At dinner I spoke tersely but politely to my father.

"Oh God oh God."

"Feels good, huh? What a tight asshole you got, fucking tight

How long he rammed his finger in and out, I didn't know, little

asshole." but he stopped abruptly and said, "Thanks, pretty boy."

When the conversation dipped into silence, however, my

mother glanced uneasily at her plate.

Him. And he was gone.

What did I learn? It's certainly better to have a finger rammed

up your ass in the back room of a leather bar than a bottle of

Budweiser.

Earlier, during the afternoon, I had simply decided to avoid any

conversation with my father as much as possible.

Later that night, I drove to the athletic center

with its Olympic-sized pool at the University of Maine at Orono.

I had been swimming every night since I returned to

Maine: 66 straight laps, free-style, for one mile, and then the butter-

fly until exhaustion.

That summer I was 26 years old.

After swimming, in the locker room, I stripped off my black

Speedos. When I opened the glass door to the steam room, I saw

three men sitting on the upper tier just as a burst of steam vaporized

their bodies. I sat down on the lower tier in one corner, bending a

leg up and adjusting my towel, and let the back of my head lean

against the tiled wall. I listened to the sound of the steam, watched

the haze, and inhaled the moist heat.

"Zee"-e-e mixed

with the hissing steam.

I leaned forward   peering into a mass of grayness,

looking for the sound of my name,

but heard only the increasing whoosh of plumbing.

Must have been a pipe.

I leaned back and shifted my eyes up and down.

That is the ceiling,

  that is the wall,

    that is the floor.

But I saw only gray gray gray.

And that is my hand.

I stretched it out in front of me, but I couldn't distinguish its shape in the steam until I pulled it in close to my face. I moved my fingers and stretched my hand out again, watching the shape blur. I pulled it back quickly, clenched it into a fist, and thrust it out just as I heard my name again—"Zee?"

My fist hit something soft.

"Oo-ue-ff."

I had punched someone.

I stood up. "I'm sorry, I couldn't see you, are you all right?"

"What are you doing, Zee? Fighting the steam?"

"Dr. Filburn?"

The face and torso of Dr. Filburn emerged from the steam as he leaned in close to me. He was holding a hand flat on his paunch.

"Dr. Filburn, I'm so sorry. . . . I was just—"

"I know, I know, playing with the perspective. I've done it thousands of times, though I've never quite *punched* at it before. Youth. Sit down, sit down, no harm done. As you can see I'm well protected." He rubbed his hand over his round, red belly.

I sat down again and he sat beside me.

"What brings you here?" he asked me. His blue eyes bulged like his belly.

"I swim every night."

"Every night?"

"Yessir."

"Well, two or three times a week, I try to play a game of rac-
quetball, but I like the steam bath most of all. Quite relaxing."

I nodded.

Dr. Filburn, a tall man in his mid-fifties, had a thin, high voice.
He was as bald as Picasso in his old age, although Dr. Filburn had
hairy nostrils and bushy eyebrows. He was an art historian at the
University and owned two art galleries, one in Portland and one in
Boston.

He started picking at his thumbnail.

I sighed.

"Long day, Zee?"

"In a way."

"Did you work today?"

"I work every day, Dr. Filburn."

"That sounds like paradise to me."

"Paradise with a final act—it won't last long."

"It can last as long as you desire it."

I laughed. "Until my savings run out, and then I'm kicked out
of Eden."

"Why?"

"I have only so much money. I can get through this summer,
but I'll be broke by October or November. Then I'll have to take on
some kind of job, like my father says."

"You'll make money selling your artwork."

"What?"

"You sell your collages," Dr. Filburn said, studying his thumbnail, "you make money."

"Enough to keep going?"

"I should hope so."

"But I haven't sold anything yet."

"You will."

"Do you think so?"

"Zee, in two months, Portland will be swarming with New Yorkers and Bostonians. I have regular customers and know their taste and their pocketbooks. The six collages I plan to exhibit, I plan to sell."

"Do you really think they'll sell?"

"Would you like to make a friendly wager?"

"I'll believe it when it happens."

"That's the only time *for* belief. Make as many collages as you can. You're talented. Don't doubt yourself."

"I don't know if I can not *not* doubt myself."

"Doubt is the internalization of external disapproval."

I looked steadily into his bulging, blue eyes.

"Let me ask you one question, Zee, and don't think before you answer—just answer."

I nodded.

"What is the one sensation you feel as you're working?"

"Astonishment."

I gained a much better sense of the role my grandfather, Gregor Matejcic, played in Yugoslavian politics when I enrolled in a course at Georgetown University called History 374: "Slavs and European Fascism."

"Then you're an artist."

"Let us begin in February 1939, with Prince Paul replacing Premier Stojadinovic with Cvetkovic," Dr. Daigle said, beginning his dreaded "Friday Q & A Session"—a class period devoted to random, rapid-fire questions to test the students' reading, comprehen-

sion, and class notes week to week. Students could not check notes
or books. "Why did this happen, Melanie?"

"Chief Minister Matejcic," she responded, "believed that
Stojadinovic stood in the way of a resolution with the Croatian demands and persuaded Prince Paul to replace him."

"What were these demands?"

"Essentially demands for greater autonomy."

"Yes, Melanie," Dr. Daigle said. "Croatia maneuvered constantly during this period for independence. The Croats believed
that independence could be realized through Fascist ideals. Was this
a wise choice on Prince Paul's part?"

"Yes, sir, because Cvetkovic and Macek, who was the head of
the Croatian Peasant Party, reached a compromise in August 1939,
resulting in a single Croatian *banovina* that included most territories
of the Croatian population."

"That's correct, Melanie," he said. "Thank you. Now, Zee,
there were five major figures of power in Yugoslavia at this time.
Who were they?"

My stomach tightened when I heard my name, but I had studied
my notes thoroughly the night before. "Prince Paul, Premier
Dragisa Cvetkovic, Vladko Macek, exiled Ante Pavelic, and Chief
Minister Gregor Matejcic."

"Of these five figures, who were Anglophiles?"

"Prince Paul and Chief Minister Matejcic."

"What were the implications?"

"The Axis powers did not trust them."

"Whom had the Axis powers trusted?"

"Stojadinovic."

"What were the implications?"

I knew I had missed a beat. Dr. Daigle repeated a question only when the answer was not wrong but not on track of what answer he wanted. I fumbled in my mind for a moment. "The Axis powers turned their attention to the exiled Ante Pavelic."

"That's right. And where was Pavelic?"

"In Italy."

"Yes, thank you, Zee. Now, Glen, what organization had Pavelic formed?"

And the questions and answers continued. What a strange sensation it was to sit in a classroom and listen to my professor and classmates discuss my grandfather as a historical figure. My grandfather had clearly stood for democratic principles in a confused time of dictatorships, Fascism, nationalism, and Communism.

"Now that we have covered the facts," Dr. Daigle continued, "we can now interpret them—speculate and surmise. Jonathan, why do you suppose Hitler felt threatened once Stojadinovic was replaced as premier?"

Jonathan answered and Dr. Daigle turned again to me. "Now, since we have Chief Minister Matejcic's grandson in class, I want to ask him why his grandfather never returned to Yugoslavia in 1945, after King Peter transferred his powers to the regency under Tito's command? Zee?"

I didn't know how to respond.

"Is that too personal a question, Zee? Would you rather someone else answer it?"

"Yes, sir."

"Melanie?"

"In 1945 Matejcic would have been 60 years old," she said. "I believe age affected his decision to—"

"That's not true," I interrupted. "Excuse me, Dr. Daigle."

"That's fine, Zee."

"How could he possibly have survived under Tito's command?" I asked.

"Your grandfather was a fighter," Melanie said. "Other exiles returned and voiced opposition to Tito."

"But it wasn't his age, Melanie. He was a vigorous old man. We used to walk for miles and miles through fields and woods. The unremitting cruelty of that time is what broke my grandfather. He loved his country, but everything he had worked for had been dismantled and discarded in a matter of months. Months! He watched his fellow Croats slaughter the Serbs, including my mother's family. He could not return to such a country.

"Shortly before he died, he told me a story about the night he and my family escaped from Dubrovnik. There was a storm at sea that night, tossing their boat up and down in huge waves, and he had to place all his trust in that boat to keep them alive. That night he thought the sea represented all the torment and evil in the world, and that the tiny boat represented all his values and his beliefs.

Yugoslavia in 1980 was a Communist country, officially called the Socialist Federal Republic of Yugoslavia, a federation of six peoples' republics: Serbia, Bosnia and Hercegovina, Macedonia, Slovenia, Montenegro, and Croatia.

Then he thought that man in the world was like that boat in the sea. At that point, he leaned over the edge and vomited—he realized he no longer had a country."

It is necessary to destroy in order to create.

It is necessary to create in order to destroy.

My parents called.

"This isn't your telephone number, Zee," my father said.

"Oh, for God's sake, Mico," my mother said. "Zee, honey, are you all right?"

I said that I was, told them about my bicycle accident, and explained that Matthew was going to take care of me until I recovered.

"And who is Matthew?" my mother asked.

"A good friend, Mother."

"Oh." A pause. "And is Matthew a friend of yours from college?"

"No, I didn't meet him at school."

"Oh." Another pause.

My father asked, "And I suppose you were biking to a job interview, is that correct?"

"Oh, Mico, leave the poor boy alone."

"Just keep that in mind, Zee. September is just around the corner."

I convinced my mother that she didn't have to fly down to Washington to look after me.

The next night I called the escort service again.

"Hello, Denny, this is Zee."

"Zee?"

"Zee, from last night. Mark?"

"Oh, yeah, yeah, well, was Mark what you were looking for?"

"Yes."

"No complaints?"

"None at all."

"So what can I do for you?"

"I'd like to hire Mark again."

"Sorry, he's not working tonight."

"He's not?" My disappointment was evident.

"No, 'fraid not. But we do have Brian available and Jimmy."

"No, no, thank you."

I held the phone in my hand until I heard the squawk of disconnection. I dropped the handset in the cradle. At the end of August, I turned my attention to job hunting. Not working tonight. My face tightened. Within two weeks I was offered a position at the National Archives. Vacantly I stared at the room. I was stunned by the official offer, since competition had been so keen, but I accepted immediately. Absence walked around the furniture. I would be working closely with Miss Claudine H. Doin, Assistant Archivist.

I phoned my parents.

"Oh, Zee, that's wonderful," my mother said. "And you'll actually be working with history."

"It's incredible," I said. "They have documents dating as far back as the Revolutionary War."

"And what are the terms for advancement?" my father asked.

"What's that, Papa?"

"What are the terms for advancement?"

"Oh, Mico, he hasn't even started yet."

"It's something that has to be considered," my father said. "Do you know, Zee?"

"Well, not really. I mean, I assume you advance."

The next night I called the escort service again.

"You *assume* you advance? In most cases, yes, that you can assume. But some government jobs lead to a wall and that wall is it. You want to be sure that this job leads to a door that opens into other possibilities."

"Zee," Denny laughed. "How are you?"

"Yes, Papa."

"Fine, fine."

"And how much did you say the starting salary was?"

"What can I do for you?"

"Is Mark working tonight?"

"Let's . . . see," he said, teasingly drawing out his words, ". . . is Mark . . . working? Hm. Oh, yes, he is."

"He is?"

"But he's booked solid."

"What?"

1) Pornography

"Just kidding.

What is pornography? Would you like to set up an appointment?"

According to the dictionary, *pornography* is defined as follows: "Written, graphic or other forms of communication intended to excite lascivious feelings."

"Yes."

The key word in that definition is "intended."

What if it fails in its intention?

The first pornographic movie I ever saw was at a straight movie theater in Washington called the Olympia Theater. Does it cease to be pornography? I biked to the theater in a black tee shirt, Georgetown athletic shorts, and sneakers. The joke falls flat.

I paid my five dollars, walked through the lobby to the auditorium, pushed past the maroon drapes covering the entrance, and couldn't see anything except the color-pulsation of the movie screen. Is it still a joke? In the dark I groped down the aisle until I finally sat down in the center, one seat in from the aisle seat.

My eyes adjusted slowly to the darkness, and I could see a handful of men scattered here and there. Some were smoking cigarettes, despite the "No Smoking" sign at the back of the theater. I lit a cigarette and noticed, in the flash from my match, a man on my left sitting three seats away from me. He was staring at me.

The movie was highly graphic but not well-made. The actors

and actresses, reasonably good-looking, staggered through various sexual positions, but the men were not my ideal of fantasy. How could I possibly be aroused by watching men I did not find attractive?

The joke was falling flat.

My eyes roamed through the movie theater again, and I saw that some men were now sitting next to each other. I watched one gray-haired man stand up halfway and scuttle to his right two seats to sit down next to this man hunched down in his seat.

A man sat down in the aisle seat next to me, his hands moving restlessly on his knees. I noticed he wore a wedding band. I glanced over at him and smiled. He looked away, startled, and stared at the movie screen.

"Hi, how're ya?" I whispered.

"What?"

"How are you?" I repeated slowly.

A strange expression crumpled his face. He stood up and moved down four rows. That was odd.

I glanced over at the man sitting three seats to my left and smiled the slightest smile (from habit, without meaning)—in a moment, he was next to me.

The least stimulus produced the most response.

He must have been thirty years old, with a meticulously trimmed mustache and long, thin fingers. He said nothing to me, but after a moment he dangled his right hand off the armrest and let it brush against my thigh. When I did not move my leg, he brushed his fingers again against my leg and then placed his hand on my thigh.

I stared straight ahead at the movie screen, didn't utter a word, didn't move my leg: *I did nothing*: which is to say I said: *Continue.*

I did not pretend his hand was not there. I did not attempt to touch his hand or move my leg, so his hand would *remain* there. I know now that the *lack* of response, initially, is desirable.

He massaged my leg and then pressed his hand into my crotch. All this time, I kept my eyes fastened on the movie screen—a bright rectangle of fucking flesh. I did not move, though my penis hardened at his touch, the necessary point of response this man desired. I kept still so that what was happening happened in this highly isolated manner. He pulled my erect cock from the side of my shorts, stroking it. From the corner of my eye, I saw that he bent his head forward to look at its shape and size. What was I to this man? A hard object.

How much more is visible?

Nothing more than an erection, broken off from my body and held in his hand—a mere fragment.

All that summer in Maine, I worked steadily at collage after collage after collage.

So I sat there immobile, watching a pornographic movie, while this man masturbated me.

Each morning my brain, my hands, and my eyes trembled.

What did I learn? If you're right-handed, be sure to sit on the left side of a man in a movie theater if you want to masturbate him.

To consummate.

I failed. I succeeded. I continued.

I was alone, active, wretched, and overjoyed.

As I manipulated pieces of paper over the surface of a canvas, sometimes I laughed.

That summer I also had recurring dreams of flying. Naked, I leapt into the endless skies and skimmed swiftly over cities and farms, rivers and forests, hills and mountains. My mother's name was Emila Ivancic Matejcic. When I saw friends or family, I somersaulted and turned in the blue air above them, laughing and shouting joyously. She owned and managed an antique shop in downtown Orono. Their astonished eyes followed each turn, each dip, each rise. She was a small, thin, trim woman in her mid-sixties with a sophisticated face and dark, watchful eyes. With the greatest ease, I moved upward or downward—this power to fly was my privilege, my will, my desire.

She always pulled her thick pearl gray hair into a chignon at the back of her head. She was vain about her hair—with a straight back and an erect head, she walked to show it off. Of its gray color now, she was as proud as she had been of its almond color when she was a young woman.

I was in her shop one afternoon, in late October, when a truckload of goods she had bought at auction in Boston arrived. A local boy worked for my mother three days a week when she had furniture to be stripped, cleaned, and stained. She had a good reputation, since antique dealers from all the major cities in New England visited her shop on a regular basis.

Closely she watched every box and piece of furniture as it was unloaded, checking each item off a master list she had.

The workmen dropped an old, battered sea trunk on the floor.

"Be careful," she said sternly to the men.

To me she said, "Now, look at that old trunk. I saw one once in a Boston shop, cleaned and polished, for $1,200. And that one was dated only circa 1920. This one dates anywhere from 1875 to 1890. An estate sale. An old Scots family."

"It's from Scotland then?"

"I hope so."

"Locked tight."

"But I have the key."

She placed a skeleton key in my palm. I didn't think such keys existed, except in old vampire movies.

"Have you opened it yet?" I asked.

She shook her head no.

When I unlocked and opened the lid to this old, battered sea trunk, a stale odor of fidelity and linen made me cough.

"A dress," I said, pulling out a mound of yellowed material.

"Not a dress," my mother said, "a wedding gown. Look at that embroidery."

"And here's the veil. Look, Mother."

Solemnly we both gazed inside at the remains of a wedding bouquet,

maroon petals

scattered on a small satin pillow.

"My God, look at this," I said, removing a daguerreotype of a bride and groom. I turned it over. "The sixth of June. 1892." I handed the picture to my mother.

"It's a trousseau," she said.

"What's this?"

I removed a bundle of letters, tied in faded red ribbon.

I read outloud the address written on the top envelope: "Maida Tay, 16 Coventry Road, Glasgow, Scotland."

I untied the ribbon, opened that envelope, and removed the letter.

"24 April 1888. Dearest Maida, Forgive my not writing"—I glanced through the rest of the letter to the signature—"This is a love letter, Mother. From Thomas, in America."

My mother and I stared at the trunk, the letters, the yellowed wedding gown.

Something   awkward turned in my chest.

I opened another letter.

From Thomas.

"These are all love letters," I said.

My mother and I were both silent for a long moment.

"Now, the name is Maida Knox."

I opened that letter—from Thomas.

"They must have married. This is from New Bedford."

I read quickly through the letter.

"He's buying fishing gear. He's a fisherman."

"There must be a hundred of them," my mother said.

I held the skeleton key in the palm of my hand. "Maida saved them all."

The antipodes of the body, the heart, the mind.

"She must have loved Thomas very much."

Later that afternoon, my grandfather and I walked the fields and woods behind our house.

"Do you want these letters?" I asked.

Layers of old ice and frozen snow, at least two feet thick, covered the land; also, that morning, two inches of powdery snow had fallen.

"What would I do with them?" she said.

"Where are we going?" I asked.

"When we get there, you will know," he said.

He pulled me along, holding my blue-mittened hand. I was wearing brown rubber boots, a red nylon parka, and a black scarf. The hood of the parka was pulled tight around my face, and the scarf was wrapped tight around my nose, mouth, and throat.

"But, *Djed*, it's so cold."

"The walk will be warm, Little One."

Through the frozen fields, a cold wind tagged along, kicking up high swirls of fresh snow. Acres of white fields, rising gently before us, swerved into one another and blurred into the edge of the distant, dark woods—white against black.

My grandfather, a short man with a thick chest and a thick beard, marched toward the woods. An old, baggy brown overcoat bunched up over his shoulders and back, making him look thicker than he actually was. His stubby nose buttoned his face together. Vigorously, he sniffed at the cold air, his nostrils dilated, tufts of gray hair sticking out. His hazel eyes, magnified by his gold wire-rimmed glasses, were moist and golden in the winter light. He peered straight ahead with an undaunted expression like some character marching through the frozen steppes in a Chekhov short story.

"I'm cold," I whined.

"Walk, Little One, walk."

I walked and walked, feeling the tingle of body heat trapped in the folds of my long underwear.

Snow spiraled up in front of us.

I slowed down almost to a stop to watch the upward-rolling twist of snowflakes, but my grandfather tugged me straight into it.

With my head bent backward, I looked up at the snow as it vanished into the cold, gray, windy sky.

Again he tugged me, impatiently, and my head wobbled back into place.

In the distance I could see a cluster of birch trees in the woods, long silver streaks quaking in the wind. A barbed wire fence separated the woods from the field, and the gate to the tractor trail stood next to the birch trees.

"Where are we going, *Djed*?" I asked again.

"Do not worry."

"Where are we *going*?"

"Do you know where you are?"

"Yes."

"Then you are not lost?"

"No."

"Then do not worry."

"But—"

"If you know where you are and are not lost, then you will always know where you are going."

I did not like it when he talked that way—declarative riddles.

When we reached the cluster of birch trees, I studied the silvery coils of bark curling from the thin trunks. I waited for him to open the latch to the gate, so we could walk through. Instead, my grandfather hoisted me up under the arms over the barbed wire fence and set me down on the other side.

One of my mittens snagged on a barb.

I stared at it, hanging there on the barbed wire fence, a bright blue shape floating in the February afternoon.

My damp, warm fingers in the winter air instantly turned dry and cold.

Baffled at having been picked up, I watched him as he unlatched the gate and walked through. He plucked the bright blue shape from the fence and stuffed my hand back into it.

"Never seek a gate until you have to and then avoid it," he declared and then grabbed my mittened hand again, and again we walked, now along the tractor trail into the darkening Maine woods.

The tall white pines took our figures.

The uppermost branches, moving in a strong wind, whispered above our heads. Our steps crunched in the frozen snow.

My grandfather slowed his pace, as though he now felt protected by the trees and the enclosing branches after having walked exposed though the open space of fields.

"Smell that, Little One."

I looked up at him.   We stopped.

He inhaled deeply, that thick chest expanding.

"The snow, the cold, the trees," he said.

I sniffed once through my scarf.

"She died on this day," he went on.

I studied the reflection of the branches in the round lenses of his glasses.

"On this day." Then he looked up abruptly at the swaying tree-tops and shouted, not with sorrow but with power and simplicity, my grandmother's name—"Irena!"

Just once.

The name filled the woods.

His voice—the solid, solitary voice of an old man—flew through the trees and spiraled upward into the whispering of the up-permost branches and disappeared.

The silence of the woods throbbed.

I stood there staring at the treetops as if I would find his voice snagged on a branch as my mitten had been snagged on the barbed wire fence.

His thick body trembled.

"Are you cold, *Djed?*"

He moved his eyes from the treetops to my face.

"Oh, Little One"—his voice whispered like the branches as he squeezed my hand—"not cold."

Again we walked through the pines toward the Androscoggin River.

The pines soon blended with black spruce and hemlock and

balsam fir—all trees of cold hillsides.

I edged the scarf down from my nose and inhaled the fresh smell of snow and balsam. The insides of my nose hardened quickly in the frigid air.

The snow, the cold, the trees.

The wind plucked at the icy light, but my grandfather and I continued to walk.

Soon the sound of the river mingled with the sound of the wind.

The late afternoon light, drained of color, had deepened to a slate gray as we emerged from the woods on the riverbank.

We stood on the riverbank and watched the dark, wide, slow-moving river, its edges frozen into silver scallops.

My grandfather released my hand and folded his arms over his thick chest. "This section of the Androscoggin is just like the Sava River in Croatia."

He gazed straight across the river at the opposite bank as though searching for something.

I saw my blue mitten floating again before my eyes and wondered why we were watching the river. My black eyes snapped bright with the cold. I shifted my weight from one foot to the other. "*Djed*, is this where we're going?"

"Little One, how old are you?"

"Seven."

"Seven years old. Do you know how old *Baba* was?"

"Seventy-six."

"Seventy-six, yes, seventy-six *long* years."

"Why long?"

"Long because long."

"I don't understand."

My grandfather sighed. "Because your *Baba* was a gypsy. And you know what a gypsy is, don't you?"

I simply looked at him and did not respond. Gypsies were dark and mysterious and told your future in a crystal ball.

"Do you know what I am?" he asked.

"My grandfather."

He chuckled. "Yes, that too, but from what country do I come?"

"Yugoslavia?"

"That's right. I am Yugoslavian because I was born in Yugoslavia and you are American because you were born in America."

"So *Baba* was born in Gypsy?"

He studied my face for a moment with delight. "No, she was born in Yugoslavia."

"Then she was a Yugoslavian, too?"

"No and yes."

I squinted at my grandfather.

"*Baba* was a gypsy who was born in Yugoslavia, but many people did not think she belonged to the country. Gypsies are a nomadic people. Do you know what 'nomadic' means?"

"Moving from place to place?"

"That's right, gypsies are wanderers. They are a proud and dignified people. Your great-grandparents, however, *my* mother and father, did not like your *Baba* because she was a gypsy."

"Why?"

"Religious beliefs, cultural status, racial purity."

I shook my head at all the terms. "Purity?"

His voice became reminiscent. "And they did not want me to marry her."

"But you did."

"I did, Little One. I did because I loved her. It did not matter to me that she was a gypsy."

"Was that why it was long?"

"That's part of why it was long."

"And the Nazis made it long, too, right, *Djed*?"

"You do listen, don't you?"

I nodded vigorously.

"And when you get older, you'll read."

"Those books in your room?"

"Yes, those books, other books." My grandfather shook his head. "The Nazis and Fascists made life long too. During the Second World War, *Baba* and I had made a pact—an agreement together—to commit suicide if we fell into Hitler's hands. *Baba* would have been killed automatically just for being a gypsy and I would have been killed automatically just for supporting Macek in the Yugoslavian Cabinet."

I didn't quite understand everything he was saying. "But you and *Baba* escaped, with Mother and Papa."

"Yes, after two months of hiding and moving, we finally got out. But so many did not. I never realized how ugly and how cruel the world could be. We escaped in a small boat out of Dubrovnik, late at night, during a storm."

And it was then that he told me the story about the sea and the boat and the vomiting.

He fell silent.

I peered across the river at the opposite bank and saw a cardinal perched on the branch of a flowering laurel.

Perhaps he had been looking for birds when he had looked across the river.

"Look, *Djed*!" I yelled. "A cardinal."

I pointed.

"See? Do you see it?"

My grandfather nodded.

The bird, a sharp-edged shape set against the whiteness of the snow and the slate gray light, was a startling red—a sudden, brilliant patch of color.

"Look, there's the female"—I pointed again—"on the ground."

A buff-brown bird hopped in the snow.

The male cardinal let out a cry and flew upwards, and I lifted my eyes to follow its movement as did my grandfather.

The female cardinal flew upwards too.

Both birds flew across the river toward us, then swerved away and alighted on the branches of a larch, upriver on a high section of the riverbank that dropped ten feet to the water.

The birds together let out slurred whistling sounds.

I darted from my grandfather and ran toward them.

I ran and ran and huffing reached the tree and looked up into it.

The female cardinal let out another slurred whistle, then flew away into the dark, snowy woods. The male cardinal cocked its head and eyed me for a moment and then it, too, flew into the woods.

On the ground, near the base of the tree, I noticed a single red feather.

I pulled off one of my mittens and picked it up, studying its bright red feather shape.

"Zee," my grandfather said, reaching me. "Why so fast?"

"To see the cardinals."

My grandfather gazed approvingly at me.

"Look, *Djed*," I said, holding up the single red feather.

My grandfather gazed at the feather, his eyes suddenly moist.

"The cardinal left that for you, Zee. It is a gift. Do not ever lose it."

I stared at the feather.

"It is a gift," my grandfather repeated, "and a secret at the same time."

"A secret?" I asked, looking up at him. "What secret, *Djed*?"

"This afternoon," he answered.

I watched him step close to the edge of the riverbank to look down again at the river. I looked back at the feather.

I heard a cracking sound and my grandfather called out.

I looked up but didn't see him.

I rushed forward and looked out over the edge, the red feather floating down the side of the riverbank.

My grandfather clutched at a shrub and some ice-encrusted rocks at the river's edge.

The feather settled near the shrub.

His boots were in the water, and he kept trying to pull himself up, but one of his legs didn't seem to work.

"*Djed!*" I screamed.

His face was pale and he had lost his glasses.

"Zee?"

"*Djed!*"

"Do you know where you are?"

"Yes."

"So you are not lost?"

"No."

"Then go home and tell your father what happened. I cannot move."

The icy ledge of snow at the edge had cracked under his weight, and he had pitched forward, somersaulting the ten feet to the river.

My grandfather broke his knee.

A bright blue shape floating in the February afternoon.

Peary went on his first Arctic expedition in 1880 and was struck year after year after that with what he called Arctic Fever—a restless longing for the battles against the great white desolation.

Maida Tay and Thomas Knox were both Scots from Glasgow.

The frigid water soaked his feet and legs, freezing him, and hypothermia had set in. My grandfather caught pneumonia and died three weeks later.

They had become engaged in Scotland, but Thomas had emigrated a year before Maida, so he wrote her a letter once a week to describe the New Land and his work as a fisherman and the love that ached in his heart, filled his eyes, sang in his soul; how he read *her* words of love over and over, rejoicing in the fact that she was his. Then she emigrated and they were married. There were seven more letters written over the next year (1892-1893) from New Bedford, when he had traveled there to get fishing equipment.

Then the love letters stopped.   Had marriage killed the love?

Had he simply tired of writing love letters?

Had they simply never been separated again?

Did she travel with him?

I sat propped against my pillows in bed.

The letters were spread out on my blue comforter.

I gazed at the yellowed paper, the blue ink, the masculine script.

3) Exhibitionism and voyeurism.

Had he been lost in a storm at sea? Did some strange disease kill him?

What is exhibitionism? A form of sexual gratification through the display of one's genitals.

I had all his love letters. But where were hers?

What is voyeurism? A form of sexual gratification through observing the display of another's genitals.

I stared at the envelopes and stamps and letters in the white light from my reading lamp, their edges sharp against the blue of my comforter.

Go-go boys (in most cases, also hustlers) danced in the Potomac House seven nights a week for the pleasure of boy-watching patrons.

How is it that the heart is the locus of love?

On the main platform stage, a go-go boy, deeply tanned with bleached-out white hair,

in zebra-streaked boxer shorts,

spun and whirled,

turned and twisted.

At the bar I ordered a gin and tonic while this other go-go boy, dressed only in sneakers and a jock strap, gyrated on the bartop and snapped his leg straps, one-two-one-two, in time to the music.

In the main room, I sat down at a table against one wall. On the main platform, the go-go boy shed his zebra-streaked boxer shorts. As I sipped my drink, he dropped them on a man's head, and, stark naked but for his white socks, danced and shook his erection in the faces of the gawking crowd before jumping down.

Another go-go boy, dressed in a tuxedo, jumped up on stage as the other dancer jumped off.

"Do you mind if I sit here?"

I looked up. "Not at all."

Tugging at the sleeves of his *Georgetown Hoyas* tee shirt, a fat middle-aged man wheezed, sank down in the chair, and clapped his whiskey sour on the table. He rubbed the back of his neck, then tugged again at his sleeves. His fish-like eyes moved constantly in his round, pale face.

"Willya look at that?" he said, his eyes jerking toward the platform stage.

I looked more intently at the go-go boy.

"A tuxedo! Can ya believe it? Who cares about a tuxedo?"

"Part of a fantasy?" I ventured. "The well-dressed man?"

"Oh-h-h, yeah yeah, but who cares about a tuxedo?"

I shrugged my shoulders.

"No one cares about a tuxedo. You want skin, flesh, movement."

At this point, the go-go boy had removed his jacket, tie, and shirt.

"Well," I said, "there's some flesh for you."

"Yeah, but he can't dance, doesn't know how to move. Does he even *know* his body?"

He wheezed again and pulled again at the sleeves of his tee shirt. He sipped his whiskey sour.

I pulled the lime wedge from my drink and chewed it—my face tightened from the tart taste. I looked around the room and noticed a small platform wedged in the far corner.

"What's that for?" I asked.

"What?"

"That little platform in the corner."

He blinked.   "For us."

"For us?"

"Yeah. Y'know, if ya feel like dancing,

"Dance," I said, "like they're dancing?"

ya can dance."

His eyes stopped moving.   "Sure, if ya feel like dancing, ya can dance. That's the guest platform."

"Does anyone ever dance?"

"All the time."

"No one's dancing now," I pointed out.

"It's early still." He twisted around in his seat to look at the
wall clock. "It's only eleven forty-five. This your first time
here?"

"Can you tell?"

"First time, last time, all the same. Never changes." He
sipped his drink again. "I've been coming for years." He belched,
ogling the go-go boy as he peeled off his jockey shorts.

"Well," I said, standing, "I'm going to get another drink."

"Catch ya later."

As I stood at the bar ordering another gin and tonic, my
eyes roamed through the bar picking out all the handsome men.
Would any of them jump up on the corner guest platform and
dance? Perform a guest strip-tease?

Along one wall, hustlers stood in sullen nonchalance in
denim jackets and tattoos. Would any of those Simple Simons
start dancing to show their wares?

I leaned against a wall in the main room and watched this
cute man in a white painter's hat. Distantly, I hoped he would
hop up on the guest platform and dance.

I glanced up at the go-go boy, a clumsy teenager now with a
well-exercised body.

I began to wonder if anyone would ever guest dance when
the man in the *Georgetown Hoyas* tee shirt jumped up and

started shaking his potbelly to the disco beat. Imitating Jackie Gleason, he shuffled about the small stage and pulled off his tee shirt in one easy motion.

His round, pale face beamed with satisfaction.

He strutted to the music with abandon.

He swiveled and hopped.

He rolled and shook.

How well he synchronized his movements with the music.

Slowly he removed the rest of his clothes.

Those sitting around him clapped and cheered his boldness, his daring, his unself-consciousness. In my mind, I did the same, impressed by this display of unconcern for his body, so unlike the trim young men hired to dance. I couldn't take my eyes off him.

When I did glance around the room, I saw that everyone else was watching him, too, much to the chagrin of the clumsy teen-ager with the well-exercised body.

All attention in the room had turned

The next morning I spray-painted a six-foot by three-foot canvas a powder blue. Using Thomas's letters, over the next few days, I created a collage out of his love for Maida.

to the fat, middle-aged man.

"That's Andy," a man next to me said.

"Andy?"

"Yeah. Dancin' Andy. Every Saturday night, he gets up there. After he dances, other guys lose their inhibitions, get up and dance too."

"Have you ever?" I asked.

When my mother saw the collage, she wept.

He hesitated. "Once. When I was really loaded."

"What's wrong?"

I sipped my drink.

She shook her head. "Nothing's wrong. It's touching, Zee. Is there a title?"

What did I learn? It's not the body but the attitude toward the body that seduces the on-looker.

"Love Letters of Thomas."

My mother took an unusual interest in this collage, describing it to my father and how we had found the love letters in an old, battered sea trunk. She insisted that he look at it.

My father gazed at it critically.

He moved close to the surface, his hands held behind his back, studying the letters.

"Do you think such intimacy should be placed on display?"

"What?" I said.

He turned around to face me. "Do you think something as private as a love letter should be used like this?"

"Oh, Mico," my mother said, her annoyance evident.

"I'm quite serious."

"I think an artist can choose his materials," I said.

"And you think this is proper material?"

"If you have respect for the material, yes, it is proper."

"I don't think you have respect. It's callous and insensitive."

"I don't think you understand," I told him.

An age of innocence.

My father left, his face sour. I shook with anger and dejection. My mother tried to comfort me and told me that she thought the collage beautiful, a beautiful tribute to their love.

In 1980 AIDS had not yet even been named.

How dare he judge my motive or my ability like that?

Nonetheless, I could not work for three entire days.

Lice, scabies, urethritis, proctitis, prostatitis, herpes, worms, shigella, campylobacter, amebiasis, hepatitis, syphilis, gonorrhea.

Medicine conquered all.

My parents, my three older sisters and their husbands attended my graduation ceremony at Georgetown University.

Penicillin: the wonder drug.

I planned on staying in Washington to find a job, but I wanted my summer free. My father argued against it, but my mother persuaded him to take care of all major expenses until September, at which point I would actively hunt for a job.

Until then I hunted for men.

The summer of sex.

The 1970s liberated gay men. In many cases, the act of sex was considered a political act. Gay men defined themselves through sex.

An age of innocence.

While at Georgetown, I was a studious young man, quiet and reserved. I had gone out to night clubs when I was a senior and had had a few one-night stands, but I was, basically, inexperienced in the arena of sex.

I wanted to go places I had never gone before

and I wanted to do what I had never done before.

I wanted to explore my sexual territory.

I wanted to create my sexual territory.

I wanted to destroy my sexual territory.

After graduation, I moved to Dupont Circle, the Greenwich Village of Washington, D.C.

I rented a one-bedroom apartment on the top floor in a four-story building at the corner of 20th and R Streets.

From my two dormer windows,

I watched men march up and down the streets.

That summer I bought a ten-speed Raleigh and biked twenty or thirty miles a day, up and down the streets, around the monuments, out the bike path into Virginia or out the towpath into Maryland.

That summer I smoked cigarettes.

That summer I smoked pot.

That summer I tried poppers.

That summer I read endlessly—19th-century French and Russian literature: Balzac, Hugo, Sand, Dostoevsky, Tolstoy, Chekhov.

I would wake in the morning, make a demitasse of espresso, and read until my legs ached to bike.

That summer I wooed guilt.

If my conscience said, "No," then I actively pursued that action.

My upbringing had to be attacked.

I had to destroy values to create values.

I would not passively accept the morals of Maine.

That summer I viewed my actions as *questions*: to answer and to define.

That summer I viewed my actions as *experiments*: to discover meaning and to uncover instincts.

I never felt remorse because each failure as well as each success constructed my moral castle.

What do you say to a young man dying?

The castle of becoming.

That Monday I marched into the National Archives once

again employed and studied the Peary painting before going into my new office.

That summer was the start of my creation and the start of my creation began with the redefinition of sex, sexual behavior, sexual attitudes, and sexual response.

Miss Doin had had the office fixed up with lamps, desk supplies, a new office chair (rising and falling at the touch of a lever), and an additional table; an IBM computer access terminal had also been installed.

What was *considered* improper, I first attacked.

I sat down at my desk, turned on the desk lamp, and stared at the cardboard boxes in the corner. Miss Doin knocked at the door.

What was improper? 1) Pornography, 2) Anonymous Sex, 3) Exhibitionism and Voyeurism, 4) Pederasty, 5) Sado-masochism, 6) Transvestism, and 7) Prostitution.

"Good morning, Zee," she said, smiling broadly, with her red-painted lips. She held a blue book in her hand and a black three-ring binder.

"I was just glancing through these," she said and handed me the black three-ring binder. "That is the Society's record of what's in those boxes. Apparently, it turned up just before they sent the material over. Not all the boxes are accounted for and the description of the contents is rather sketchy and incomplete in most cases." She handed me the blue book. "That is Peary's own account of his North Pole expedition. There are a few other studies on Peary you should read as well before you start. The computer access code for our Peary material is on your assignment sheet and you have complete freedom to examine all the Peary material we have on the second floor."

Miss Doin was not one to waste time. And with that, she wished me luck and repeated how grateful she was that I had agreed to return to the National Archives and tackle this task.

I glanced through the black three-ring binder, and the information was indeed sketchy and incomplete.

The North Pole, the title of the Peary book, was bound in rich sapphire blue covers.

On the title page, in the faded blue ink of a fountain pen, were the words "Property of Gilbert H. Grosvenor."

Grosvenor was the patriarch of the National Geographic Society, a staunch supporter of Peary's every single polar expedition and a defender of his claim to the North Pole. He had, in fact, written the introduction to this book.

Arctic Fever: a restless longing for the battles against the great white desolation.

So I started reading.

What were the considerations? 1) Color, 2) Shape, 3) Size, 4) Juxtaposition, 5) Material, and 6) Surface.

The first week would be reading, studying, and familiarizing myself with Peary and his polar expeditions.

"The lure of the North! It is a strange and a powerful thing. More than once I have come back from the great frozen spaces, battered and worn and baffled, sometimes maimed, telling myself that I had made my last journey thither, eager for the society of my kind, the comforts of civilization and the peace and serenity of home. But somehow, it was never many months before the old restless feeling came over me. Civilization began to lose its zest for me.

Morning.

I began to long for the great white desolation, the battles

with the ice and the gales, the long, long arctic night, the long, long arctic day, the handful of odd but faithful Eskimos who had been my friends for years, the silence and the vastness of the great, white lonely North.

Birds started.

And back I went accordingly, time after time, until, at last, my dream of years came true."

The darkness cracked.

And the light climbed up the pointed firs into the wide summer sky.

Tingling with the cool green dawn, I woke, and at once images, shapes, colors, and lines dashed through my brain and fingers.

I also had a morning erection.

I kicked off the sheet and comforter to masturbate. I rubbed my right hand in circles over my chest as I gripped my balls with my other.

Pale transparent gray over a dark green patch.

                         Two ragged white strips then side by side.

I pulled at myself.

                   Side by side requires verticality.

I came.

              Verticality breaks central focus.

I showered and dressed.

I drank a cup of black coffee, ate some toast and yogurt.

              Then the plummeting movement is halted by the rising mass of gray.

I walked up the macadam road toward my parents' house.

I passed a neglected apple orchard, a field swimming with

Black-eyed Susans, and a large pasture with a small herd of graz-
ing Holsteins.

Black and white and burning orange.

Pain is burning orange.

I examined the sunshine that rippled along the edges of a tall
hemlock in the side yard of their house, a farmhouse built in
1784.

The hemlock, from this angle, formed a perfect
triangle.

Behind the roof of the house, I saw the tops of black spruce,
shining in the sky.

The old abandoned hay barn, attached by an ell to the house,
had become my new studio.

Shape must sacrifice color.

I slid open the great doors to let the morning light fill the
barn. In the center of the barn stood a white canvas, ten feet by
eight feet. The canvas was tilted, however, so the corners were
the sides; the lefthand corner had been cut out, leaving a triangle
of open space, and that corner had been affixed to the top
righthand corner.

Then I began.

Where to begin?

I began by staring at the white shape that
vaguely resembled an iceberg.

Where to begin?

That was the single most important question
since the rest of the collage swirled into shape from the initial
placement of a ragged piece of paper or an acrylic line or a
splotch of paint.

The first mark committed me, challenged me, dared me.

An image of dark green and pale gray colors striking each other near the lower righthand corner of the canvas mixed and blurred and erupted up along the canvas edge in plaster and carbon fibers.

What I imagined was in practice exceedingly complex. To turn not only the image in my mind but the sensation spinning in my face into a discrete aesthetic object was an act of responsibility.

All the materials I needed were lined up on the picnic table at my side.

I stared at the whiteness, squinted.

I tried to imagine what the finished collage would look like: to follow the steps to get there, though I knew that in the composition the collage assumed a certain freedom of its own.

I took three steps back, frowning.

Two steps forward.

One step back.

I picked up a long narrow piece of Bristol paper, spray-painted green, and held it out in front of me, turning it from side to side.

Then I set it back down and picked up a different piece.

For two hours, I stared at the huge white canvas, picking up and examining different pieces of paper. Finally, I unscrewed a jar of paste, slapped some on the back of one ragged piece of paper, and placed it on the canvas.

The movement began.

Piecing together my collage. Assembling and unifying. Forming a whole out of fragments.

I pasted and placed.

With a paintbrush, I painted dark green lines and dark gray

lines.

I splotched paint here, there, outlined strips of paper.

I molded and shaped and moved the pieces over the surface of the canvas.

I squished palmfuls of plaster over the color.

I set carbon fibers in the plaster along its edges.

I pasted, placed, squished, and painted all morning until noon.

"Zee?"

The green must respond.

"Zee?"

The green must respond *passively* in this area or otherwise—

"*Zee?*" my mother said emphatically.

I turned from the canvas toward her, my eyes focusing on her figure, holding a tray. I stood on the third step of a stepladder, my hands stained an avocado green. I held a long, ragged strip of green paper. "Hello."

"Your lunch," she said, setting the tray down on the card table. "Ham and Swiss on rye, a banana, and iced tea."

"Thanks."

I finished pasting that piece of paper in the upper righthand corner, then hopped off the stepladder.

"Have to wash my hands," I said, waving my fingers in front of my face.

"I should hope so," she said, smiling.

While washing my hands in a deep metal sink in the far corner, I watched my mother study the collage and then noticed the envelope in her hand. She knitted her eyebrows together. How puzzled—yet delighted—she was at some of them! She loved to look at them as much as she loved to look at me as I worked, even for a short while, since I preferred to work alone.

She had been amazed at my energy. I had converted the barn into a studio little over a month ago, yet I had filled it with supplies, tables, empty canvases, finished collages. It was as if I had had a dozen collages complete in my mind and had only to get the materials to transfer idea to medium in rapid succession.

Just last week, Dr. Max Filburn visited me and agreed to show two of my larger collages and four smaller ones at his Portland art gallery this August. When I told my parents, my mother had clapped her hands and could hardly contain her pleasure, while my father merely grunted assent. My father thought this sudden interest in collage was a great waste of time—I could have been earning "work experience" at the National Archives.

My mother stood directly in front of the collage with her head tilted to one side.

"What do you think?" I asked.

"Why is that corner cut out and why is it tilted like that?"

"It had to be."

"Had to be tilted and the corner cut out?"

I nodded.

"Well," she said, "the green and gray seem to leap off the canvas at the side since the white is so very white."

I smiled distantly, observing the colors.

"Had to be tilted," she muttered then smiled broadly. "I like it. So far, that is."

"You're my mother."

"And your mother appreciates contemporary art. Does it have a title?"

"Hmm, no, not yet." I picked up half the sandwich and took a bite.

She sat down in a ladderback chair next to the card table.

"Oh, here's another letter," she said, holding it out. "Matthew again."

"Hmm." I took the letter from her. Displeasure somersaulted in my stomach.

"Maybe you should open this one, Zee."

"It'll be the same old thing," I said, flipping the envelope over.

"Maybe not."

"I doubt it." I dropped the letter on the card table, then picked up the iced tea, and drank half of it.

"But you can't keep sending every one back."

"Why not? He keeps writing them."

"Maybe you should just write him a letter, Zee."

"That's just what he wants, Mother, can't you see? A response. And then another and another and before you know it, we're all mixed up again and I can't deal with that right now. I want to work on my collages and nothing else. If he keeps getting the letters back, then maybe he'll get *my* message."

"Do you think that's fair?"

"When has love ever been fair?"

She sighed. "I don't know, Zee. It's just that he's been writing about two or three times a week. Have you read *any* of his letters?"

I finished eating one half of the sandwich and started the other. "The first one," I said, chewing. "None after that."

She shook her head. "Oh, well, it's your affair."

I took another bite of the sandwich.

"Is the sandwich good?"

"Great."

"Which collages does Max want to show?"

I turned around and pointed to an eight-foot by ten-foot collage in the distance.

"Oh . . . now what's that called?"

"*First Light, Orono.*"

"Oh yes."

I pointed out the other collages that Dr. Filburn had chosen to exhibit as I finished eating my lunch.

"Well," she said, "almost one and I have to get downtown." To re-open her antique shop. She picked up the tray and examined the collage I was working on once again. "You know, Zee, I think you should put a little more gray in the upper lefthand corner, don't you think?"

I glowered humorously at her. She laughed then walked back to the ell.

I stared at the letter lying face down on the card table. I turned it over, studied the handwriting, picked up a red felt-tip pen, and wrote in large block letters RETURN TO SENDER over my address.

I paced back and forth in front of the collage, inspecting it. I picked up another piece of green paper and climbed the stepladder. I worked steadily until my arms sagged and my eyes burned.

"Enough."

I dragged the stepladder to the side of the picnic table. I sat down and scrutinized the collage. Not bad. Not too much more to do.

I washed up, closed the great doors, and shut down my barn studio for the day. When I stepped outside, I gazed at the far back fields, rippling with golden wheat, the air sweet with its fragrance, and held my face up to the mid-afternoon sun.

On the back patio, my father, dressed in tennis shorts, sat in a white Adirondack chair under the violet shade of a black ash. A tennis racket and a can of tennis balls were on the ground next to him. He had a glass of lemonade on one armrest and a small pile of papers on the other.

My father, a mathematics professor at the University of Maine (calculus, abstract algebra, and algebraic topology), frowned at a clipboard on his lap. His reading glasses were perched on the end of his long nose and his salt-and-pepper hair fluttered over his broad forehead.

"Hello, Papa."

My father raised his eyes and tufty eyebrows, wrinkling his forehead, and said, "Zee," as he scratched an X next to an answer.

"Homework?" I asked.

"Tests."

"Oh."

I folded my arms over my chest and looked aimlessly about the back yard. He marked a grade on the test, circled it, placed it in a manila folder at his side, and removed another test from the pile on the armrest. I went inside to get a glass of lemonade.

I sat down in the other Adirondack chair and let my gaze travel once again over the wheat fields. The scratching of my father's pen sounded like a wasp.

"Did you play a game of tennis after classes?" I asked.

"I did not. Every court was occupied. Dan and I are going to try later on, before dinner."

"Is it that busy during the summer session?"

"Apparently."

I sipped my lemonade. Apparently. Of course. Silence.

My father asked, flatly, "How did it go today?"

"Really well," I said, leaning forward. "I started a new collage this morning in green and gray, with plaster. I hope to finish it by Friday. It's a big one and I tilted it so the corners are the sides and cut one corner out."

"Did you."

"Yes . . . I don't know why exactly. Not yet anyway. For some reason, the canvas had to be tilted and that corner cut out. Turned. Just to alter the angles somewhat, the perspective. A jolt."

"A jolt."

I sat back. My father marked another grade and circled it. I sipped my lemonade.

"You really think this is a complete waste of time, don't you?" I asked.

"Not a *complete* waste of time, but I can't see any future in it. Now, you *had* a future—"

"At the National Archives?"

"Yes. At the National Archives. It is part of the federal government and you had a perfectly good position, with a future."

"I don't want a future."

"What do you want then?"

"A present."

"Oh, Zee, don't start in with some Buddhist crap and nonsense."

"It's not nonsense. I wanted to make collages."

"You *were* making them."

"Oh sure. At night for a couple of hours. I didn't have enough time. I didn't have enough space. And Matthew and I—"

"Don't mention his name," he said sternly.

"Why?"

"Had it not been for him, you wouldn't have been so unhappy and left your job."

"That is not true."

"I'd rather not continue this conversation. You're here now and as soon as you recover from the problems you were having—"

"Problems? I wouldn't classify them as problems. Limitations, maybe. Dissatisfaction, but not problems."

"Well, whatever you want to call them, I call them problems. And as soon as you get this collage foolishness out of your system, you can start to look for another job. Maybe you could teach at your old prep school? You can't make collages the rest of your life."

"Why not?"

"Because your savings won't last that long."

"You and I don't think the same way at all."

"It doesn't matter what way I think or what way you think. What matters is that you have to have an income. And if you don't, then believe me your thinking will soon become more like mine."

I stood up. "We'll see how my thinking becomes."

I walked through the back yard, hopped the split-rail fence, and jogged along the edge of the wheat fields. My heart beat with murderous thoughts as I walked alongside the barbed wire fence toward the birch trees.

When I reached the tall white trees, I glanced at the latch on the gate.

Crows screamed.

The golden wheat rippled

        in a sudden breeze.

The crows flapped over the field,
black marks

in a dark blue sky.

My face was bright with anger and confusion.

Crows over wheat field.

Are we not all Pearys?

The black wings flapped my anger into perspective.

"Hey, Zee," Glen, my college roommate, said one night while studying, "it says here that your grandfather married a gypsy. You never told me that."

I shrugged my shoulders.

Why should I expect my father to understand what I'm doing? Mother does. Matthew does. But why does he keep writing letters when I've sent every single one back? He knew I wanted a clean break.

"So you have gypsy blood in you?" he asked, looking at my black hair and dark eyes.

Sharp black lines in a dense blue.

"One quarter gypsy, one quarter Croatian, and two quarters Serbian equals one American."

The crows slid into the horizon.   Vanished.

"Isn't that kinda exciting?"

I set my hand on the top of the post and hopped over the barbed wire fence to the other side. The tall white pines took my solitary figure. A cardinal darted through the uppermost branches.

"Having gypsy blood?"

"Well, yeah, I mean, more than being just plain old Irish or Scottish."

"I never really thought about it."

"But I mean it's—" He faltered. "Well, being a gypsy . . ."

"What are you getting at?"

"A gypsy's a minority."

"And?"

"C'mon, Zee. Hitler killed one million gypsies during the war."

"Gypsies were persecuted, sure."

"But think about the implications for your grandfather. He married outside his race, his class, *and* his religion. At the time that was a pretty courageous thing to do, wouldn't you say? And yet there's only one short paragraph here about it."

"About his marriage?"

"Yeah, in chapter seven. And it says he saw your gypsy grandmother the first time at the edge of some river."

"What's that? What does it say?"

"Quote. In 1915, the day Matejcic joined the Party of Rights, the day that marked the start of a long and complicated political career, he walked along the Sava River contemplating his political position and stopped to watch a caravan of gypsies making camp across the river. The music of a mandolin and the laughter of children carried across the water. He saw a young gypsy woman, standing waist-deep in the river, washing her long black hair. That gypsy woman would later become his wife. End quote."

Peary had a constant companion on every journey he undertook, a black man named Matt Henson.

"Could I see that?"

7) Prostitution. What is prostitution?

"Sure, right there, page 266. Haven't you done the reading yet?"

Someone who solicits and accepts payment for sexual favors. Male prostitution—the world of hustlers and tricks and escort services.

Selling your body.

But, more than that, selling your *time* to someone else—letting them *use* your time, your body. Which is more important?

One night I was flipping through *The Washington Blade* when I saw this two-column advertisement for "D.C.'s Hottest Men: To Satisfy Your Every Need."

"Hello?"

"Hello," I said, wondering if I had dialed the wrong number. "Is this the Metropolitan Escort Service?"

"Why do you ask?"

Evasive, non-committal, guarded.

"I saw your ad in the *Blade* and wanted to ask a few basic questions about hiring an escort. How much does it cost? How long is it for? How much time in advance do you need?"

"We have quite a few hunky men available this evening," he said, suddenly animated, all business. "Do you want someone for this evening?"

"I don't know. How much does it cost?"

"Fifty dollars the first hour, twenty-five an hour after that. We accept American Express, Visa, Mastercard, Travelers' Checks, and cash."

"I'd have to pay cash."

"Then you pay the escort. Now, what type of escort were you looking for: leather, preppy, construction worker, boyish, cowboy—"

"Preppy, I guess."

"And what are you into?"

"Pardon me?"

"Bondage, verbal abuse, water sports—"

"Oh no, nothing kinky."

"Just a good time, right?"

"Just a good time."

"Okay then. We have Brian available tonight. Brian is twenty years old, white, handsome, short brown hair, blue eyes, clean shaven, five ten, one hundred and fifty pounds, a smooth chest, swimmer's build, and eight and a half inches cut."

"Well, that's thorough."

"Does Brian interest you?"

"Well, sure he does, but could you tell me about a few more?"

"We also have Jimmy. Nineteen years old, white, cute, medium long blond hair, green eyes, mustache, five eight, one hundred and forty pounds, some hair on his chest but not much, muscular, and seven inches cut.

"We also have Mark. Twenty-two years old, white, dashingly good-looking, short light brown hair, brown eyes, clean shaven, six feet, one hundred and eighty pounds, hairy chest, smooth back, muscular, seven inches cut.

"Any strike your fancy yet, hon?"

"Mark sounds interesting. Is he really that good-looking?"

"*Dashingly* good-looking."

"Okay, then, why not Mark."

"Fabulous."

"But . . . I . . . I mean, it's one thing for you to tell me about these guys and it's another when I meet the person. What if he's not what I expect?"

"You pay a traveler's fee."

"How's that?"

"If, for some reason, you don't like the escort we send you, then you just pay him ten bucks for the time and trouble of driving over. No questions asked."

"So if I don't like Mark, I just say so and give him ten dollars?"

"That's right, hon, but you're not going to be disappointed in Mark. No one has yet."

"Now what?"

"Directions. I just have to get in touch with him. It's nine-thirty now. Would eleven be all right for your appointment?"

"Sure. And he'll do what I want him to do?"

"All our escorts are quite versatile."

I gave him my name, telephone number, and the directions to my apartment.

The telephone rang immediately after I hung up. The man at the escort service called back to verify the number I had given him.

I sat and waited and wondered what would happen.

The telephone rang again ten minutes later.

"Is this Zee?" a strange voice asked.

"Yes."

"This is Mark."

"Mark? Oh . . . hello."

"Just wanted to call to check the directions. You're expecting me at eleven, right?"

"That's right."

"By the way, is Zee your real name?"

"It's Yugoslavian. Short for Zeljko."

"Yugoslavian. I don't think I've ever met a Yugoslavian before."

His voice, watercolored with a Southern accent, pronounced each word distinctly. I confirmed the directions.

I emptied ashtrays, picked up shirts and socks from the floor, and changed the sheets on my bed. I also turned off the air conditioner—that night in August was surprisingly cool—and opened all the windows. The voices of laughing children, brakes screeching, and the smell of curry floated into my apartment.

I stood in my living room, among the furniture and the sounds, and thought how a room changes when someone enters it.

How a human figure upsets the balance of a room.

The imaginary planes alter.

The room must accommodate an additional presence.

And this presence is not a friend, not a relative, not an acquaintance, but a prostitute—a man hired by me for sex.

Under my control. To buy someone. To control someone. For an hour.

But was it my control? Didn't he have *me* under control since I have to pay *him* for services rendered? That the services rendered did not exist were it *not* for him? Was I using him or was he using me?

I decided to have a cup of espresso. Then I thought would *he* want a cup of espresso? Or perhaps a drink? What did I have to drink? Some red wine, vodka, gin. Could he even drink while working?

At ten-thirty, I kept looking at my watch and waiting for the buzzer to sound. I sat in my reading chair—this ancient green wing chair I had bought at the Salvation Army for five bucks—reading, or attempting to read, *The Wild Ass's Skin*. I would read two paragraphs, stand up, step to my window, and search the street for a slow-moving or a parking car. Then I would sit again, open the book, and read two paragraphs.

At eleven-thirty, I wondered if he would ever show up.

I called the man at the escort service who assured me that Mark would be there, that he probably had trouble with traffic or locating the building.

To buy sex.

What did that mean?

To give someone money and tell him to suck my cock for five minutes, bite my nipples, and then lie down so I can fuck him.

And while I fuck him to recite a poem by John Ashbery.

Is this the type of control I want? Is that the type of control others want? Or is it, simply, lack of control?

No one has been yet. Disappointed with Mark. Had by other men, used by other men, shared by other men. One body touched by many strange hands.

That excited me.

But what type of person, what psychological framework does it require to sell your body to strangers? To perform sexual acts on cue? If he can't perform, do you still have to pay?

The hustlers leaning against the wall at the Potomac House. What if Mark is like one of them? Sullen, listless, bored.

Dull, plain, average. *Dashingly* good-looking. I should trust the escort-service description? All their models *have* to be hunks, beautiful, knock-outs, Mr. Americas, Mr. Universes.

A horn honked.

What about body lice, gonorrhea, and scabies?

Are the escorts clean? Sex with anyone at any time?

The buzzer buzzed.

I jumped out of my chair, *The Wild Ass's Skin* dropping to the floor.

I buzzed him in.

I stood at the top of the stairs.

This man bounded up the staircase two steps at a time, turned the corner on the third landing, and stopped when he saw me. A puzzled expression crossed his face.

"You're not Zee, are you?"

I stared at this man on the staircase. "Yes. I am."

He bounded up the steps with the intensity of Van Gogh colors, stood in front of me, eye to eye, and held out his hand. "I'm Mark."

I shook his hand.

"I'm going to have to meet more Yugoslavians if they all look like you."

"Well, come in."

"Nice place. One bedroom?"

I nodded.

He bent over, picked up the book from the floor, and read outloud, "*The Wild Ass's Skin.*" He placed it on the side table. "Philosophical studies. May I use your telephone?"

"What did you say?"

"Telephone. I have to call in."

"No, about Balzac."

"Oh, *The Skin.* Falls under what he called philosophical studies. He grouped his books into three categories: manners, philosophy, and analysis. But I really have to call in since I'm running late. Denny gets very very nervous very very quickly."

"Over there by the window."

"Thanks. Oh," he said, turning to me, "am I okay?"

"Excuse me?"

"Am I okay? For you? Am I what you expected?"

"You're not what I expected, but you are definitely okay."

He smiled. "Thank God."

I watched him sit down in the chair and dial the escort service.

I realized I was still standing in the doorway, not having moved, my hand tight on the doorknob. I closed the door and sat down in my reading chair, comparing the description of Mark over the telephone with the person here before me. It was the difference between reading in a catalog that Picasso painted five women in *Les Desmoiselles d'Avignon* and seeing the painting. How empty and meaningless the telephone description had been!

I was stunned by his good looks.

Strong ankles, finely shaped calves, solid thighs, broad chest, well-formed biceps.

Van Gogh painted stars in *Starry Night*.

A light blue short-sleeved Izod shirt, white cotton shorts, a dark blue cloth belt, top-siders—Mr. Mark was prepped out, clearly in the *role* of a preppy type.

Can you see more?

He sat in the corner of my room like a still-life painting—a study in shades of brown: skin, hair, eyes. His tanned skin was smooth and dark. His hair, the color of burnt almonds, cropped short on the sides, fell across his forehead. His bright eyes were the color of sepia.

He had the nose of Monet and the mouth of Pollock.

He had his head bent at an angle that accentuated his strong neck and the line of his jaw.

As he talked on the phone, his entire face responded to the words he spoke, forehead furrowing and unfurrowing, eyes widening and narrowing, jaw moving and unmoving.

His face was painted with irony, passion, and intelligence.

One fact was clear: this man was a handsome man.

One other fact was clear: this man was a hustler.

A hustler who reads Balzac.

One other fact was also clear: the name *Mark* did not fit the person. The title of this painting was wrong.

He kept looking at me as he talked.

"No, no trouble with the directions," he said. "Friday night traffic. Everything's cool. Yes, he is. I'll tell you later." He glanced at his watch. "I'll give you a call in an hour, about one-fifteen, okay? Sure . . . yes, yes. Talk to you."

He sat up straight in the chair, facing me, his face knotted with questions and confusion, and folded his arms over his chest.

He said, "Well."

"Well," I said.

"Denny, the guy who runs this service, said you were young and that you sounded hot over the phone."

"Is that unusual?"

"Of course it is," he said, his face clustered with incredulity. "Our clients aren't usually young. And if someone *is* young, he's not exactly what you would call 'hot.'"

"Oh."

He looked me straight in the eye. "You're not a cop or anything, setting me up?"

"No," I laughed. "Hardly."

He regarded me suspiciously.

"I'm really not," I said. "Believe me."

"O-kay," he said cautiously.

"Why do you call the service when you get here?"

"Protection. I call in at the start of the hour and at the end. If I don't call back, then Denny knows something's wrong."

"Makes sense."

"One other item. Denny said you would be paying cash."

I nodded.

"I have to see the cash to stay. Rules and regulations."

I removed the money from my pocket and set the bills on the table next to Balzac. "So you've read *The Wild Ass's Skin*?"

"Couple years ago."

"I just started it tonight."

"Well, I won't ruin it for you," he said, "unless you would *like* me to ruin it. Some people enjoy that."

I looked back at him. "No. I don't like that. I like to turn the page and be surprised."

"To be surprised. Is that what you look for?"

"That's part of what I look for."

"That's what I look for, too."

"Would you like a drink? Wine or something?" I asked. "I mean, *can* you drink while . . . working?"

"Sure, I can have a drink," he replied, "while *working*. But I'd prefer something else."

"Orange juice?"

"That's fine. Now, you understand that this is for an hour unless you pay more?"

I handed him a glass of orange juice. "I understand."

"What I mean is, your hour has already started. It starts when I phone in."

"I understand."

"Denny said this sounded like your first time."

"This *is* my first time."

"Well," he said, standing up.

I stood up and sighed.

We regarded each other like two animals confronting each other in an unknown woods.

"Take off your shirt," I said.

He shook his head, no.

"No?"

"You have to make the first move, baby, not me."

I pulled off my shirt and stepped over to him. My fingers touched that jaw.

"How's that?" I said.

"Perfect."

"Now, take off your shirt."

At the end of the hour, he called the escort service and jotted down another name, address, and telephone number.

I noticed the fifty dollars were gone.

And then he was gone.

Peary said the first thing he did upon awaking was to write these words into his diary: "The Pole at last. The prize of three centuries. My dream and goal for twenty years. Mine at last! I cannot bring myself to realize it. It seems all so simple and commonplace."

In the crumpled sheets, damp with perspiration and gripping, I thought reason was sliding out of my brain, dripping from my ears on to the pillows.

Possession.

I sighed and panted. I trembled. My heart slipped.

When I opened the first box, I found some black-

and-white photographs in a manila folder.

Reason squared its solid shoulders and marched around the room as my body plunged into a naked sleep with well-dressed dreams. Possession.

There was one striking, close-up portrait of Peary: a study in physiognomy.

He was old. A sheepskin hood, trimmed with white foxtails, surrounded his face. Brooding eyes, dark with defiance, smoldered with disappointment. The deeply furrowed glabella, the brow etched with lines, and the heavy eyebrows pressed the face into a severe frown. The large nose and prominent nostrils, the thick mustache and short, stubbled, gray-streaked beard lengthened the face into stern disturbance.

This was not the portrait of a happy man.

I placed the photo at the time of his 1906 failed expedition to reach the North Pole, though he had achieved the "farthest north" at 87 degrees 06 minutes. When I flipped the photograph over and read the date and place written on the back, I was astonished—it was taken on the ship *Roosevelt,* soon after he returned from the North Pole.

That didn't make any sense. Perhaps the person identifying the photograph was wrong. I did have the impression, however, that I had seen the picture before. I searched through books and magazine articles until I found it in a *National Geographic* article his daughter had written about him and the American flag.

Again, the date was his return trip from the North Pole.

Peary's daughter described the photograph: "No elation, only the fatigue and nervous tension of a thousand miles of sledging show in the face of the man who just found the North Pole."

But there was more than fatigue in that face.

I thumbtacked the photograph on a bulletin board above my desk. I wanted to have this man watch me as I sifted through his belongings.

Looking through the box again, I was amazed at the disarray: torn papers, papers tied up with twine, packets tossed on top of one another, loose sheets of papers, and papers held together with rusty straight pins (the equivalent of paper clips way back then).

I picked up a few of the loose papers and looked through the dates: 1893, 1890, 1901. Computations and figures covered most of these papers. Still, I couldn't imagine that these papers had been thrown in here in such a manner with such an important historical figure.

The North Pole has no size. It is a mathematical point: no length, no breadth, no thickness. It is the geographical pole—not the magnetic pole—and is simply the point where the imaginary line known as the earth's axis intersects the earth's surface. Ninety north.

I stared into the box at the torn and yellowed sheets of paper, while this slow excitement stirred in my fingertips at the thought of arranging and piecing together this miscellaneous material into a coherent whole.

An imaginary point.

To organize it for posterity, as Miss Doin would say.

Possession.

One day in November, my mother said she had something to show me down at her shop.

I glanced at the Peary photo.

When we got there, we went into the back work area. "Don't worry, ol' boy, you're in the best of hands here," I said to the photograph. She showed me an old oak rolltop desk, wallpapered on the sides with green flowers and painted yellow in front.

"Take a look," she said.

I was confused. Did she want me to have it? I rolled back the top and examined the writing surface. "Is it very old?"

"The Forties."

I opened the deep bottom drawer. Inside was a bunch of loose papers, and then I noticed a bundle of letters.

I turned to her.

She nodded.

"Have you looked at them?"

She shook her head. "No."

I removed the bundle and read the address on the top letter: Elizabeth Deering, 17 Franklin Street, Portland, Maine, USA. There was a military APO. I opened the envelope and read that letter. Date: March 24, 1943. From: Edward Deering, her husband, fighting in Italy, describing the country and the war and how much he loved her and how much he missed her and how much he wanted to be home.

I started another collage the following morning—*Love Letters of Edward.*

That second bundle of love letters started my "love letters" series.

I searched through all the antique shops, Salvation Army Stores, thrift stores, and second-hand shops in Orono and the surrounding towns. I traveled down to Bangor and farther down to Portland. I looked through newspapers for advertisements of old desks and filing cabinets and estates sales.

All in all, I found six bundles of love letters, dating from 1910 to 1964, and made six additional collages so that I had eight in all, a perfect exhibit for Dr. Filburn. *Love Letters of Thomas*, my first one, remained the oldest grouping.

But the curious fact, in general, was that all the love letters I had found were from men.

6) Transvestism. What is transvestism? To dress in the clothes of the opposite sex.

The women had kept them. I did not once come across any love letters that a man had saved. One day I hoped to find a bundle of love letters that a man had kept.

Most transvestites are heterosexual.

Only a small segment of the gay community cross-dresses, and that small segment cross-dresses with severe ostentation.

On Saturday night, I went to Don't Look Now, a small nightclub on M Street, to watch a drag show.

The night was rainy, damp, and cool, so I wore my white windbreaker.

I was sitting at a table along the back wall, sipping a scotch and water, when the house lights dimmed.

The host, a man with a Clark Gable mustache, stepped on stage wearing an Annette Funicello wig, a white lacey slip, black garters, black nylons, and black stilettos. Turning his back to the audience, he cooingly asked into the microphone, "Are my seams straight, Frankie?"

Someone in front yelled that they were.

"Well, honey," he shouted, "that's probably the *only* straight thing in here tonight!"

The audience cheered.

"I suppose you want to see some *real* tits and ass, don't you?"

The audience cheered again.

"Well, let's bring on the legend that gave new meaning to 'my cup runneth over,' Don't Look Now's one and only—or should I say *two* and only—our very *own* Misssss Jayne Mansfield."

The spotlight staggered to the side of the stage as a drum roll boomed.

From the edge of the curtain, only two breasts emerged.

The audience burst into laughter and clapping hands.

The music began and this man, wearing a platinum blond wig and a white clinging gown, stepped from behind the curtain and sashayed to center stage. He looked remarkably like Jayne Mansfield. The audience laughed and clapped as she danced and pouted and struck various poses. Camp it up. After Jayne Mansfield disappeared into the wings, Bette Davis, Joan Crawford, Carol Channing, and Lana Turner all appeared on stage.

Then the stage lights dimmed, and a solitary blue spotlight shone on center stage. The host set the microphone stand in the middle of the blue circle of light, looked out at the audience, and whispered, simply, "Sabrina."

The audience clapped and clapped and cheered as this gorgeous black woman, tall and slender and thin-hipped, wearing a strapless silver-sequined gown with a slit up one side to mid-thigh, slipped into the blue light.

The clapping and cheering increased enthusiastically.

I wasn't sure if she were a man or a woman.

Sabrina bowed her head and blinked her liquid brown eyes. When she looked up, her eyes flashed with mischief.

She raised both

hands to her neckline,

           crossed her wrists,   and
spread
        her long fingers to form a fan,

                              her long fingernails
painted silver.
        Her black hair fell

                    in a wild mass like seaweed on her thin
shoulders
                    —a black sea nymph.
        She kissed the microphone and the band started to play.
        Then she sang.
        Her voice was toffee ice cream.
        Sabrina sang a few lively songs by Aretha Franklin and Diana
Ross, and then eased into Morgana King and Sarah Vaughn, but
she did not attempt in any way to imitate their voices—she sang in
her own remarkable voice.
        "Tonight," she said, breathing deeply, "I'd like to sing a song
I wrote the other day called 'Photographs of Photographs.'"
        I groaned inwardly, anticipating that the song would fall
down dull and flat.
        Surprisingly, the lyrics were clever, the rhythm was simple,
and the melody was snappy.
        To complete her set, she kicked up a snazzy "Fever" of
Peggy Lee fame.
        When she finished singing, the audience stood in applause. I
stood, too, clapping and clapping, for she truly was remarkable. I
still could not believe that Sabrina was a man, so convincing was
her illusion of femininity.
        She glided off the stage.
        The house lights came up, and the host announced a twenty

minute intermission until the next show. Disco music filled the bar, and a few men started to dance.

I walked over to the bar to order another scotch and water.

I saw Sabrina

moving through the crowd toward the bar,

kissing this one and that one,

cooing, "Thank you thank you thank you."

She stood next to me and said to the bartender, in a man's voice, "Eddie, darling, a White Russian, please. A drink for the exhausted."

"Anything for my Sabrina," Eddie said.

"You were quite sensational," I said. "And I enjoyed the song you wrote."

She turned those liquid brown eyes on me and studied my face for a long moment.

"Thank you, darling, I appreciate that. Have you ever seen my act before?"

"No, first time here."

"I didn't think I recognized you. You get to know all these tired faces after a while."

She held out her hand.

Taking her hand, I said, "I'm Zee."

"Zee?"

"Z-e-e. It's Yugoslavian."

"Rea-ea-lly, darling," she said, her eyes bright. "My name's Sabrina. It's transvestism."

We both laughed.

She lifted her leg, the slit of her gown opening, and pulled a card from her garter. "Here's my card, darling, in case you ever need an entertainer."

"Thanks," I said, reading it. I zippered it into the front pocket of my white windbreaker as Eddie, the bartender, set down a White Russian on the bar.

She sipped her drink, gazing at me.

She had a remarkably well-defined face, despite the heavy make-up, which was heavily applied obviously for stage purposes and strong lights. The skin on her arms was the color of maple syrup.

"Let's sit down, handsome. I've been standing much too long and these heels kill my calves."

Her gown rustled as she sat down and rustled as she crossed her legs, one long brown thigh exposed as the slit in her gown opened.

I sat down and lit a cigarette. "How long have you been singing here?"

"Too long now. About six months."

She sipped her White Russian.

As Sabrina and I talked about her work in the nightclub, my mind wrestled with thoughts about the stylish manner in which she strutted on stage and dipped into song and with her being a drag queen, a transvestite, a crossdresser.

I gazed at her face.

This man is *dressed* like a woman.

This man is pretending to *be* a woman.

This illusion of femininity.

This unreason of appearance.

This reality of masculinity.

This unreality of masculinity.

If I am sexually attracted to a man and not to a woman, then what about a man

dressed as a woman? The image of a woman? Am I only *not* attracted to the image of a woman,

not a woman?

I found myself *not* being sexually attracted to Sabrina, even though I knew she was a he.

Confusion nestled itself in my chest.

How would I react to a woman dressed as a man? Would I be attracted to the *image* of a man, to the *illusion* of masculinity?

"Darling? Darling? Are you there?"

I blinked my eyes and my head snapped straight.

"You're going to burn your fingers, sweetheart."

I looked down at my cigarette and crushed it out.

"Have you been drinking much?" she asked.

"No, no, I only had a couple of drinks."

Raising her pencil-thin eyebrows high, she studied my expression.

I laughed. "I was just thinking, that's all."

"Oh."

The host in the Annette Funicello wig reappeared on stage in a yellow polka-dot bikini. His hairy chest and hairy legs brought roars of laughter from the crowd.

"Do you have to sing again?"

"Oh, no, once a night is enough. At this point, all the faggoons have had so much to drink that they want to laugh, not listen to songs. Those tacky Craig Russell imitators can flop around the stage and make them laugh."

All of a sudden, I asked, "Well, would you like to go out for a cup of coffee somewhere?"

Coquettishly, she tilted her head. "Of course, darling."

"But where?"

"How about Enrico's?" she suggested. "That's only a couple of blocks down on M Street."

"Fine with me."

"Okay, but it'll take a few minutes for me to change." With a flourish, she stood up and left the table.

I wondered how long it would take to remove all that makeup and stuff.

I wondered what she looked like as a man.

Why did I even ask her out for a cup of coffee?

Do I want to sleep with her?

With him?

What would it be like to sleep with a drag queen?

On stage I watched Judy Garland appear, dressed in an outfit the colors of the rainbow. Liza Minnelli followed her on stage, dressed in an identical outfit. The two stomped around the stage, hurling insults at each other. Every time Judy Garland tried to sing, Liza Minnelli interrupted. Finally, they started to fight, slapping each other and pulling at their clothes.

During the fight, Sabrina returned. "Ready?"

I looked over at her as surprise dislocated my face.

"What's the matter, darling?" she asked, turning to the side. "Is my skirt too tight for your taste?"

Black high-heeled shoes, black nylons, a black leather skirt, a turquoise blouse trimmed with flounces, her hair pinned up on top of her head.

"Uh . . . no," I stammered, "not at all."

"Then let's go, darling."

She held out her arm.

Slowly I stood up and laced my arm with hers.

How can she go out dressed like that in public?

Groans and moans and regrets ricocheted inside me over my rash invitation for a cup of coffee. I can't believe I'm going to walk downtown, arm in arm, on a busy Saturday night, with a man dressed in drag.

Embarrassment seeped into my face.

At the nightclub exit, I hesitated.

"What *is* the matter, darling?"

"Nothing. Nothing at all. I just have to use the bathroom before we go. Excuse me."

I hurried to the men's room. Fortunately, no one was there. I leaned against the sink and stared at my face in the mirror.

What *is* wrong with walking arm in arm with a man dressed in drag?

Nothing.

Nothing wrong with it.

Wrong, wrong, wrong, wrong—tear that word out and rip it apart.

It's acceptable to listen to her sing, acceptable to stand in applause, acceptable to talk and laugh in the nightclub—but trespass on the outside world? No.

Oh no.

Don't cross

   the barbed wire fence

           to the straight side.

I am going to walk down M Street with a drag queen and sit in a restaurant and have a cup of coffee. That's all. To hell with

what others think—their expectations, their rules, their morals—
that is precisely what I have been determined to reject. I've been
to porno theaters, leather bars, go-go bars, parks, discos, and city
beaches—all gay ghettos. Enclosed within those boundaries, *we*
are protected against *them*.

But do not cross that boundary line.

It is necessary to cross that boundary line.

I walked over to the urinal. While I was pissing, the door
opened.

"Darling, are you ill?"

Startled, I turned my head to her. "What are you doing in
here?"

She closed the door behind her.

I zipped up my pants, flushed the urinal, and turned around.

She held my eyes with a steady gaze. "Are you having second thoughts about accompanying a drag queen for a cup of coffee?"

I held her liquid brown gaze. "What do you think?"

"I think it scares the shit out of you."

I studied the set expression on her face. "You're right. It
does scare the shit out of me. But let's go anyway."

She seemed pleased at my answer. "Are you sure?"

"As sure as I can be, Sabrina."

"Let's go then," she said confidently, her eyes shimmering.
"And let me give you a little advice, darling—scare the shit out
of *them*!"

With that we marched, arm in arm, out of the men's room
and out onto M Street.

The rain had ended. The wet sidewalks shone. The city air
smelled of night and traffic lights.

As we marched down M Street, those who did glance at us did so without derision, with a startled expression of admiration. Then it occurred to me that Sabrina was bewitching in her self-possessed style.

She asked, solicitously, "How you doin', darling?"

"Fine."

"Truly?"

"Truly."

"I'm so happy then."

We reached Enrico's and I opened the door for her. She tilted her head slightly and sashayed into the restaurant. Customers in booths and at tables turned to admire her, whispering to each other. The host looked up from the podium, removed his glasses, and exclaimed, "Sabrina, my love, how are you tonight?"

"Enrico, darling, tonight I am *entranced.*"

"And I am entranced as usual by your loveliness. Let me show you to a table, my love."

He asked us to follow him as he made his way down the aisle.

As we followed him, customers murmured,

"Good evening, Sabrina,"

and "How are you tonight, Sabrina?"

and "Was the show a hit?"

I felt as if I were with some sort of celebrity and realized, in a way, that I was, though I had never considered it from that perspective. Was I the only person in Washington who thought she was talented, stunning, and witty? I had to laugh at my hesitation and doubt.

Sabrina did more than scare the shit out of them, she made them love her.

"Cocktail?" Enrico asked, seating us.

"Not tonight, darling."

"Very well, a waiter will be over in a moment."

I stared at her dumbfounded.

She raised her eyebrows. "Darling, you *do* have an expressive face. What's wrong with you?"

"You are extraordinary. How do you know all these people?"

"Fans, fans, fans. What can a good girl do?"

"They've seen your act?"

"Do you think only gays go to Don't Look Now? Hardly."

"I'm . . . amazed."

Leaning toward me, she whispered, "That's a good way to be."

My face shifted into admiration for this woman, this man, this outrageous human being, as I realized she was an artist.

After coffee and dessert, we stood on the sidewalk hailing a cab.

"Why don't you come to my apartment for a drink, darling?"

"I'm not sure, Sabrina."

"Then let me be sure for you."

A cab stopped, and we climbed in.

"Just drop us off at Scott Circle, darling," she told the driver.

"Sure thing, baby."

My face tightened as she unlocked her apartment door.

"Here we are," she announced, opening the door and flicking on a light switch.

A white baby grand stood in the far corner of the apartment, wedged in between a maroon Art Deco sofa and a matching arm chair. Posters of singers and Hollywood film stars covered the walls. One wall, entirely of shelves, was crammed with albums and cassettes.

She glided over to the stereo system, dropping one shoe then the other. "Is there anything you'd like to hear? I bet I have it."

"I bet you do."

"Well, darling?"

"Whatever you like."

"Oh, don't be so passive, Zee," she snapped. "Request something."

"How about Billie Holiday then?"

"No no no, too depressing. No singers. Something else."

"Prokofiev."

"Marvelous, darling, but what?"

I started to shake my head, but she glared at me.

"Okay, okay, one of his concertos."

She pulled out an album, removed the record, and placed it on the turntable. I could see that the cover had a reproduction of Henri Rousseau's *The Sleeping Gypsy*. Strong, decisive, icy violin notes penetrated the room.

"*Concerto No. 1 for Violin and Orchestra, D Major*," she said, swaying to the music. "Sit down, darling, take off your jacket. Let me get you a drink. What would you like?"

I took off my windbreaker and sat down on the plush maroon sofa, facing the baby grand. I was about to say "anything" until I remembered Sabrina liked definite responses. "Do you have wine?"

"Red or white?"

"White."

"Chardonnay, okay?"

"Yes."

She swayed into the kitchen and reemerged holding two

long-stemmed white glasses, filled with white wine, and sat down next to me, curling her legs up under her. "Here, darling."

I drank a little wine, then set the glass down on a blue-mirrored coffee table. I gazed at my blue reflection.

"So you like Prokovief?" she asked.

"Yes."

"So do I. I love all the Russian composers, except Tchaikovsky."

"I assume you play the piano?"

"Since I was six."

"Really?"

"Yes, darling, don't look so shocked. I'll play for you later."

"And you sing."

"And I dance and tell bawdy jokes. I am a multi-talented woman, darling."

"You *are* talented, Sabrina."

"In more ways than one, darling."

I felt slightly uncomfortable. "How long have you been singing?"

"As long as I've been playing the piano." She sighed and sipped her wine. "My big, black daddy is a major East Coast PR man for RCA records. Mother Bitch spent all her time on Broadway working as an advertiser. Two blacks make good in the Big Apple. Mother Bitch pushed me into piano and singing and I thank her for that. I studied voice at Juilliard, strictly classical, and graduated last year but . . . the big but . . . when I told my parents I was going to sing in nightclubs and *not* try out for some dull opera company, they were furious. They didn't spend $50,000 on voice lessons to have their son dress up in drag and sing in nightclubs, so they kicked me out. I came down here to live with my sister until I could get on my feet, which I did at Don't Look Now. And here I am. Is that enough bio, darling?"

"Enough bio."

"Good. But we still have to go through the drag-queen business, don't we?"

"What's that?"

"Come on, darling. The why-are-you-a-drag-queen question."

"We don't have to go through that."

"I'd rather go through with it now and get it over with. It's a normal question, and I can tell you're the questioning type of the human species."

The music stopped. She leaned over and kissed me full on the mouth.

"Does that scare the shit out of you?" she asked.

I didn't say a word.

She stood up to change the record.

I was strangely calm when she kissed me. I was attracted to her—to her style and to her personality, but not to her sex because she *was* a woman.

When she sat down, she asked again, "That doesn't scare the shit out of you?"

"No, because you're a woman."

A pained expression flashed through her liquid brown eyes. "Come into my bedroom. I want to show you something."

I followed her into her bedroom and she had me sit down in front of her dressing table. Different colored jars and bottles stood on the tabletop along with lipstick, compacts, eyeliners, and brushes. I stared at my image in the mirror.

"Are you game?" she asked.

"For what?"

"A transformation."

I stared at my reflection. She wants to paint my face. "You want to turn me into a woman?"

"No. No. I want you to turn *yourself* into a woman. Does that scare the shit out of you?"

I studied my face. "I don't know."

She sat down next to me. "Take off your shirt."

I unbuttoned my shirt, pulled it off, and tossed it on a chair.

"What you first want to do," she explained, "is to apply a base of face powder. Your skin is fairly dark, so try this." She handed me a compact. "Go on, open it."

I opened it and looked at the small, round mirror.

"Take the puff, dab it lightly into the powder, then rub it over your face and eyelids, ears and neck."

I held the compact and stared at my small, round reflection.

"Zee, it all comes off with a little cold cream."

A feeble smile formed on my face as I started to dab the puff on my cheek. With a satisfied expression settling on her face, Sabrina watched me as I applied the face powder.

"Don't forget your ears, Zee."

I powdered my ears. The face powder made my skin appear extremely smooth.

As I powdered my ears, Sabrina pulled off her wig and set it on a Styrofoam headstand. She had short black hair, all matted down. She picked at her hair with a long-toothed comb to lift it.

"Now, try a little blush." She pointed to another compact. "Brush it on those high cheekbones you have. Also, take that other compact and brush some powder along the line of your jaw."

As I did this, Sabrina unbuttoned her blouse, removed it, and wrapped a towel over her shoulders. She unscrewed a jar of cold cream, dipped her long fingers into it, and started rubbing the white cream on her face.

The blush added color to my cheeks, highlighting them. I set the compact down and leaned toward the mirror. I studied my dark eyes.

"Use that light blue eye shadow and some silver," she said. "Run the silver close to your eyelashes, the light blue over most of your eyelid and the silver again above that. Also, run some silver under your eyes."

Her face was covered entirely in cold cream, and she was rubbing nail remover on her fingernails.

I brushed the silver and blue on my eyelids, surprised at how much larger my eyes appeared. I picked up the eyeliner.

"Pull your eyelid like this," and she tugged at the skin near her temple, "and slowly draw a line along your eyelashes."

I leaned in close to the mirror to do this, and then leaned back to study the effect. I picked up the mascara and brushed that on, my lashes long and separate. I drew in eyebrows and applied lipstick.

While I was drawing on my eyebrows, Sabrina stood up, undoing the clasp on her black leather skirt, and undressed behind me. She sat down next to me in a white tank top and running shorts, plucked Kleenex from a box, and wiped the cold cream from her face.

I was using the lip liner when she finished wiping off most of the cold cream.

"Here," she said, handing me a black wig, "put that on while I wash my face."

She stepped into the bathroom.

I held the wig in front of me, then set it on my head.

Rubbing her face with a towel, she stepped back into the room. Then she stopped and stared at me. She draped a white bathrobe around my shoulders to cover my chest.

Behind me stood a handsome, muscular black man who said, "Zee, you're absolutely ravishing."

I gazed at myself in the mirror, or rather, not at myself, but at this beautiful woman. I studied my reflection as though it weren't me. But it wasn't me. It was a woman—a dark-haired, beautiful, dark-featured woman.

Sabrina placed her hands on my shoulders. "Zee, you make quite a woman. Look at that face. You look like some mysterious gypsy."

My grandmother's image appeared in the mirror. I was speechless and turned my eyes up at her, at him, at this man.

My grandfather Gregor Matejcic studied law at the University of Zagreb in Croatia, the northern part of Yugoslavia near the Austrian and Hungarian borders.

"Now, ask me the question."

"What question?"

"The why-are-you-a-drag-queen question."

I held his liquid brown eyes and asked him.

In 1913 he joined the Party of Rights after receiving his law degree.

"Because it's fun," he said.

"Fun?"

He smiled.

"But you don't dress like a woman all the time, do you?"

"Of course not. I dress for the shows and then I camp it up

afterwards. That's about it." He smiled again and asked mischievously, "How do you like being a woman, Zee?"

In 1915 he joined the Croatian infantry to fight in World War I.

"I don't know," I said and laughed nervously. "But I am rather stunning."

"You *are* a stunning woman," he said, "but you're also a stunning man."

"And you're a handsome man, too. But I can't call you Sabrina now."

"Call me Sutton."

That night, as a woman, I slept with Sutton.

In 1915 he also married Irena Sabljak—outside his race, his class, and his religion.

We slept together a few more times, but the sex just dropped away and we became the proverbial fast friends.

What did I learn? If you're an attractive man, then you're also an attractive woman.

In 1919 he became the Labor Organizer for the Croatian Peasant Party.

He worked closely with Stjepan Radic, head of the Party, and went to jail with him for three months for "state security reasons." After their jail sentence, he traveled with Radic in western Europe and the USSR until their return to the Yugoslavian Parliament in 1924.

In 1926 he supported Svetozar Privicevic of the Independent Democratic Party, who had reconciled his party with Radic.

In 1928 a Montenegrin terrorist assassinated Radic. My grandfather then worked closely with Vladko Macek, Radic's successor.

In 1929 King Alexander declared a royal dictatorship.

In 1934 a Macedonian terrorist assassinated King Alexander

in Marseille.

In 1935 voters elected my grandfather as a Minister in the Yugoslavian Cabinet. He continued his support of Macek and the newly formed United Opposition.

In 1941 a conspiracy overthrew the existing government and reorganized under General Dusan Simovic and King Peter, Alexander's son, now of age to rule.

In 1941 my grandfather became Chief Minister, representing Croatia, in the Yugoslavian Cabinet.

After they made camp one day, Peary climbed to the top of an ice pinnacle, strained his unwavering eyes into the whiteness beyond, and imagined himself already at the North Pole.

On April 6, 1941, Hitler invaded Yugoslavia and dismembered the country.

To claim that single geographical point for the United States.

On April 14, 1941, Hitler proclaimed the Independent State of Croatia. Hitler entrusted this new state to Ante Pavelic, a nationalist fanatic and head of Ustasa, the Fascist terrorist organization.

To fly the stars and stripes on the top of the world.

On July 24, 1941, my grandfather and his family, Simovic, King Peter, and other government officials escaped through the Middle East to London.

His patriotism overwhelmed him.

"You got a *job*?" Glen said.

After four months in London, assassination threats convinced my grandfather to travel across the Atlantic Ocean to America.

"It's only temporary."

Underneath his fox skin and caribou outfit, Peary had wrapped around his body against his sweat-scented flesh an American flag made by his wife, who had painstakingly embroidered forty-five white stars into the blue field of taffeta.

"But what about your artwork, your collages?"

"I doubt I'd be doing anything for a while anyway. It might be good for me to do something else—therapeutic."

Glen shook his head. "All this from an argument with your dad?"

I lifted my eyebrows.

"You know what this means?" he asked.

"No?"

"It means that you have to pay half the rent."

"No, that's not what it means. It means I have to find a place of my own."

I carried the books home to read, engrossed in the narrative, immersed in this fascinating quest, this epic poem of adventure, of Peary's single-minded obsession to achieve his goal.

I told Glen that I didn't want to impose on his friendship and that I had grown fond of being alone up in Maine. The truth, however, was that Glen was driving me *nuts* with his constant chatter about Madonna, movies, night clubs, and BMWs.

Peary had to go where no man had ever been. He braved the dangers and hardships and setbacks with fortitude.

I went to the Housing Office at Georgetown University and searched through the notices tacked on the bulletin board.

Each loss he turned into gain; that is, he *learned* not only from success but also from failure.

That afternoon I was checking the penciled numbers on a slip of paper with the bronze numbers on the front door of a magnificent, three-storied, Colonial Revival townhouse on S Street in Woodrow Heights. The sides of the front door and the entablature were knotted with the thick, twisted vines of a wisteria. A tall

honey-locust tree, speckled with pale green buds, shimmered in
the front yard.

Peary held firm in his eyes the four authoritative energies I
have come to respect: courage, insight, sympathy, and solitude.

I knocked the knocker and waited. Someone peered out the
side window.

The door opened a few inches.

A young man's voice, thick with a British accent, said, "Yeah,
yeah, yeah, now whut d'you wont?"

"I'm checking on the room for rent advertised at the Georgetown Housing Office."

The door opened wider.

This teenage boy, the sides of his head shaven, had a single,
bleached, foot-long spike rising from the top of his head. A black
skeleton earring dangled from his left earlobe. As his intense gray
eyes narrowed, his face crumpled into an enigma. He had a full set
of braces on his teeth. He wore a torn black tank top and black
jeans, cut off at the knees.

"Now, now, whut did yooo sigh?"

My words stumbled.

"Come, come, cat got yer tongue?"

A woman's voice called from within, "Who is it, Kevin?"

The teenage boy said to me in an emphatic American voice,
"My name is Unicorn."

"Kevin, who is it?"

A tall, attractive woman, in her mid-forties, dressed in blue
jeans and a gray sweatshirt, appeared behind the single spike. She
had the same intense gray eyes. Her short golden hair, pushed back
behind her ears, accentuated the sharp features of her face. She
held a trowel, and a speck of dirt smudged her cheek.

"May I help you?" she asked.

"Uh . . . yes, I'm checking on the room for rent you posted in the Georgetown Housing Office?"

"Oh, yes, please come in. I'm Judith McKinnon and this is my son Kevin."

"I would appreciate it if you called me Unicorn," he said in a petulant voice.

Judith rolled her eyes upward. Unicorn ran up the stairway in the foyer. She brushed a hand against her face. "He's in this Sid Vicious phase."

"It is *not* a phase," he yelled down from the second landing.

4) Pederasty.

"Excuse me, excuse me," she called upstairs, and then motioned to me to follow her down the hall to the kitchen.

What is pederasty?

She whispered, "He's really a sweet boy no matter how hard he tries not to be."

Sexual contact between a man and a boy. Modified: adolescent.

I rented the room on the third floor and moved in that evening.

One morning, wearing nylon shorts and a blue tee shirt, I biked past the Watergate Park and saw this young man standing next to his bike, gazing at the bike path and at me passing. He had fine blond hair cut short, long legs, and wore only sneakers and a pair of cut-off brown corduroy pants. I glanced back at him once, then continued on my way to the Lincoln Memorial.

In front of the Lincoln Memorial, I studied the image of the Washington Monument in the reflecting pool. Then I noticed, not far from me, among the gathering crowds of tourists, the young man standing next to his bike.

He looked at me, holding my eyes   for a moment.

I climbed back on my bike and rode along the edge of the reflecting pool to a concession stand. I bought a large Sunkist and sat down on the grass to drink it.

In a short while, on the opposite side, I saw the young man standing next to his bike.

After I finished my drink, I biked over to him. "Hi."

"Hi."

"Great day for biking, isn't it?"

He nodded once. Then he blinked and held his eyes shut for a moment, his long lashes a delicate embroidery in the sunlight. He had turquoise-green eyes. His face was lean and smooth and clean-shaven. His chest was smooth. His long legs, however, were covered by a downy mat of fine blond hair.

I estimated his age to be eighteen, nineteen.

I asked him if he'd like to go biking with me, that I had planned on going for a long bike ride.

"Sure."

"Where'd you like to go?"

"The towpath?"

"Fine."

"Out to Little Falls?"

"That's a good ride," I said.

We both climbed on our bikes and set off.

Little Falls is a good forty-five-minute ride into Maryland. The towpath runs along the Chesapeake and Ohio Canal, following the contour of the Potomac River. Within minutes, the city was left behind as we biked into a deep green July landscape—the river surging on one side and the canal placid on the other. The brown river sparkled with sunlight. The canal reflected the blue sky and green trees.

At times we biked alongside each other, watching our expressions.

At other times he biked off ahead of me. I studied his legs as he pedaled—his tensed calves, his tightened hamstrings, his taut ass.

Since it was a Tuesday morning, no one was on the towpath. On weekends, however, everyone in the metropolitan area seemed to be jogging, walking, hiking, biking, fishing, or strolling on the towpath.

The towpath seemed to belong to us that morning.

On and on we biked until the trees spread open where the river widened and rushed over itself in a series of descending rapids.

Little Falls.

We stopped.

My legs were tight and my chest heaved. Standing next to each other, straddling our bikes, we looked out at the riverscape.

"Nice view," I ventured.

He nodded and blinked, holding his eyes shut again for a moment, then languidly let his eyelids rise.   I leaned over and kissed him on the mouth.

"There's a fishing spot on that island we can go to," he said. "My dad and I used to go there when I was a boy."

When he was a boy. How long ago was that? Ten years? Twelve? We hid our bikes in the bushes, and I followed him down a narrow path that lead to a side stream. We crossed it, jumping from rock to rock, and climbed the bank on the opposite side.

"This way," he said.

Again, I followed him down another narrow path until it

opened up to a grassy knoll, a clay-red bank, and a pool of deep water. Upriver were the falls.

He sat down on the roots of a huge sycamore tree.

"You used to come here with your dad?"

He nodded.

"To fish?"

He nodded again.

"What kind of fish can you catch here?"

"Snapper, pike, sunfish."

"What would . . . I mean. . . ."

"Did we eat them?" He laughed. "No no. It was more for practice when we went on vacation up to New England or out to Oregon. Also, it was just to spend time together, sitting."

"Did you enjoy that?" I asked, imagining this quiet scene of father and son.

"Very much," he said. "I always enjoyed being with my dad."

I sat down next to him, studied the calm expression on his face, and kissed him again. He kissed me back and held me.

That morning we explored kissing: face, neck, ears, shoulders, arms, fingers.

This young man was not a novice for being a teenager.

I kissed his chest, his nipples, his tight abdomen. I unbuttoned his cut-offs and unzipped his fly. He reached down for me, thrusting his hand inside the waistband of my nylon shorts.

A fish jumped in the water.

A blue jay screeched.

A bullfrog croaked.

A boy's voice said, "This way, Dad-dy."

Both our heads popped up and, startled, we stared at the path.

As I was pulling up my shorts and he was pulling up his

cut-offs, this tow-headed boy darted into the clearing.

He stopped short, holding a fishing rod in his hand, and stared at our fumbling figures as we separated.

"Colin, where are you?" a voice from the woods called.

Mischievously, the boy smiled at us, then darted back onto the path.

"Colin, where are you?"

"This way, Dad-dy, let's go to the spot downstream."

"Okay, okay, but hold on till I get there."

We looked at each other as their voices disappeared.

"Smart kid," I said.

"A polite boy," he said. "Wanted to leave us alone."

"Colin. That's a nice name. By the way, what's your name?"

"Gerard."

"Gerard," I repeated.

"How old do you think he was?" he asked.

"About nine or ten."

"Not much more than that."

"And how old are you, Gerard?"

What do you say to a young man dying?

"Me?"

I nodded.

While I was unpacking my clothes, Unicorn knocked on my door and shuffled into my room.

"Does it make a difference?"

He was bare-chested, no hair at all on his chest—

"Just curious."

"Sixteen."

only a dark, thin curl of hair rose from the waistline of his jeans up to his belly button.

What did I learn? A full sexual experience with a sixteen-year old boy was as satisfying as a full sexual encounter in sixteen minutes.

"So what's your name?"

"Zee. Z-e-e. It's Yugoslavian."

"How do you do," he said, extending his hand. I shook it. Good manners.

"And you're Unicorn, right?"

"That's right," he said, sitting down on my bed. "It gets pretty hot up here in the summertime, but we do have central air. And you can use a fan if you want to. That's what other students have done. Are you a student?"

"No. I'm working on a special project at the National Archives. It's only for a few months."

"Top secret?"

"Not top secret."

"My dad used to work for the government."

"Did he?"

"Yeah. A lawyer for the State Department. Agency for International Development."

I nodded.

"But he's dead now."

"Sorry to hear that."

"Car accident. Three years ago."

"That's too bad."

"Yeah. I miss him. He was a pretty rad dude."

"So you live here alone with your mother?"

"My older brother lives here, too, but he's at school now. The University of Pennsylvania."

As I considered what college to attend, my father told me that my grandfather had said to him once, "I hope the Little One goes to Georgetown. Those damned Jesuits know how to knock an education into your head."

Unicorn lay back on the bed. I stopped putting away my socks and looked at him lying on the bed next to my suitcase. He looked over at me, fixed me with his steady gray gaze, and asked, "Hey, are you gay?"

I dropped a sock.   I held his eyes. "As a matter of fact, yes, I am."

"That's cool. My brother's gay."

My grandfather had taught at Georgetown for an academic year. He had become enamored of the University and its vast holdings on Slavic history. Although my grandfather had been a professor of history at Bowdoin College for the rest of his life, he had left all his papers, memoirs, and books to Georgetown.

"Stojadinovic rotted the country!" my grandfather shouted. He pounded the dining room table with his fist. The grilled squid jumped. The entire family stopped eating and lowered their eyes.

The stars and stripes and sweat.

"Moreso than Tsevelsic?" my father asked angrily.

"Yes!" my grandfather growled, standing up. "More than Tsevelsic."

"*Must* we go through this again?" my mother asked, shaking her head.

"Stojadinovic was concerned with *himself*," my grandfather continued loudly, "*not* with the Croats or the Serbs or the Slovenes. Only himself! He carried the Fascist poison into Yugoslavia when he sought German protection, molding himself into the *fuhrer* of Yugoslavia. He was mean-spirited and selfish, a nationalist fanatic."

"And the Peasant Party was not nationalistic?" my father asked.

"No! Not in the same way," my grandfather insisted, pacing back and forth now in the dining room.

"Nationalism is nationalism," my father said flatly.

"But the Peasant Party wanted a parliamentary democracy, Mico, *not* a totalitarian government. Hitler was manipulating Stojadinovic the entire time, but he was too power-blind to see Hitler's hand."

"What could the Peasant Party have done?"

"Resisted."

"You mean be murdered."

"That is one form of resistance."

"Then why didn't you stay?"

Abruptly my grandfather stopped pacing and shouted, "I *did* want to stay, but King Peter wanted me with him because he thought I would be more helpful alive in exile than dead in my country!"

"Then why didn't you return?"

Defiantly my grandfather stared at the faces surrounding the table. "How could I return after Pavelic took control of the so-called Independent State of Croatia? How could I return after the Croats, my countrymen, slaughtered the Serbs mercilessly? How could I return to a country of butchers? I no longer *had* a country, Mico, none."

Over the years and over the miles, Peary would cut out a part of the flag and deposit it in a cairn along with some written notes.

My mother, her face white and her eyes shut tight, sat weeping.

Altogether, six pieces of the flag were cut and left at various points on his marches north—two pieces in 1900 (never recovered), three pieces in 1906 (two recovered by other expeditions), and the final piece deposited at the North Pole in 1909 (never recovered).

My mother is a Serb.

All through December, January, February, and March, I searched for love letters.

Then, one afternoon, just before my mother left for an auction in Bangor, she asked me if I had looked through the attic in our own house. "There's a bunch of old crates and boxes up there from the Mastersons. We never got around to throwing them out. They're all near the north window, piled up under the eaves. And, Zee, you'll have to fend for yourself at lunchtime because I won't be back until Wednesday."

I climbed into the attic and peered at the dusty furniture, old toys, lamps, boxes, piles of rope, broken garden tools, desks, bureaus, and my old three-speed bicycle. I maneuvered through these objects and searched through the Masterson boxes: only old magazines, newspapers, and knickknacks—all possible collage material in themselves, but no love letters.

I stopped to inspect my old bicycle when I knocked over a standing lamp into a cardboard box, tearing open its lid.

Setting the lamp back upright, I noticed brilliant colors in the box.

The brilliant colors were an intricately embroidered shawl.

I lifted it out to examine the handiwork when I saw a photograph of my grandmother and grandfather in a tarnished silver frame. I picked that up and studied the stiffly posed photograph. I imagined it was taken when they first arrived in America. Both were middle-aged: he had a challenged but relieved expression on his face and stared directly into the camera, but she gazed down at her hands folded in her lap.

I removed a few ties, two shirts, a pair of cuff links, and then I saw a bundle of letters tied together.

My breath hitched, my eyes twitched, and my hands grew cold. I started to breathe slowly as I picked up the letters.

The name on the top letter was Irena Sabljak, my grandmother's maiden name.

This can't be.

That night I fell asleep flying.

In the morning, I stretched a new canvas, six feet by six feet, and spray-painted it silver and pearl white.

I sat and contemplated the canvas, moving the 38 letters and envelopes around in my head, searching for the placement of that all-important first letter at just the proper angle, the proper location, the proper and most significant point from which all the rest of the collage would emerge.

Plotting my moves.

Anticipating problems.

The following morning, I placed that initial letter on the canvas.

Then the movement began. I never left the barn studio.

I drank coffee and ate yogurt. For two full days I worked until I finished it.

At 6:00 p.m. on Tuesday in late March, I finished the collage.

When I stepped back to gaze at it, I thought this collage was the best piece of work I had done since I returned to Maine—the best piece ever.

Distantly I thought that this was not even mine—not my

work—not my hands that had realized it into existence.

Detachment hovered in the air.

My imagination had started to work *through* me rather than *with* me.

My imagination had become independent.

The lover-letters series restricted me, thus forcing me into creativity.

My skin prickled.

Something that had been me in a deep dream sense was now *not* me.

This was the first sentence: "It may not be inapt to liken the attainment of the North Pole to the winning of a game of chess, in which all the various moves leading to a favorable conclusion had been planned in advance, long before the actual game began."

Nine o'clock.

Through me not with me.

I had an appointment with Mark at midnight.

I sat down to read but could not concentrate.

I did pushups and situps.

I drank a gin and tonic and ate the lime wedge.

I lit a cigarette and paced around the room.

I turned the air-conditioner to HIGH.

I took a long, cold shower.

I shaved carefully, closely, so that my face was as smooth as possible.

I splashed after-shave lotion on my face

and neck

and combed my long black hair back from my face.

I examined my image in the mirror,   stepped back,

and studied

    my shoulders and chest.

    I dressed in a white tank top and cut-off jeans.

    I drank another gin and tonic and kept glancing at my watch.

    I sat in my reading chair, agitated, waiting for Mark.

    He did not bound up the staircase as he did two nights ago, but stepped slowly, his face impassive and flat.

    He telephoned the escort service.

    He sat slumped in the chair.

    "Would you like a drink?" I asked.

    He nodded. "I assume you have the fifty dollars?"

    "Right there, under the ashtray."

    He didn't even glance down at it.

    I spilled gin on my fingers as I poured his drink. After I handed him the glass, I sat down in my reading chair and lit a cigarette.

    "Well," I said, recalling that first uncomfortable "well" I had uttered the first time we met, though this "well" was more uncomfortable than the first.

    "Yes," he said, "well," and sipped his drink.

    "A busy

He stared at me distantly. "The usual."   night?"

    "What's the usual?"

    "Turning as many tricks as I can."

    "How many is that?"

    "What does it matter?"

    "Just curious."

    "Four . . . five, if possible."

    "That's quite a few."

"I'm quite the popular escort," he said, an edge of sarcasm in his voice.

"How did you get involved with the service in the first place?"

He sipped his drink, glancing at the bookcase on the far wall. He then trained a penetrating gaze on me and started to cross-examine me. "What's the deal? Are you writing a graduate thesis on male prostitution?"

"No."

He looked at me, his face knotted with questions. "You just called to hire an escort?"

"That's right."

"Why?"

"Why?" I repeated.

"That's right—why?"

"Because I wanted to."

"Because you wanted to? What the hell kind of answer is that?"

"I don't have to give you any kind of answer," I said, suddenly angry. "All you need is the fifty dollars, right?"

"Yeah, that's right, and all you need is the sex."

I crushed my cigarette out in the ashtray.

"Look, Zee, *why* would someone like you call an escort service?"

"What do you mean?"

"Are you in the closet?"

"No."

"Do your parents know?"

"They wish they *didn't* know."

"Then why don't you go out to Lost and Found or . . . or Rascals, that's right here in Dupont Circle. You don't have to *hire* someone. Or are you doing this because you get some kind of kick out of humiliating me?"

"How am I humiliating you?"

"You have a mirror, don't you? You know how good-looking you are, yet you hire me. You could walk into Rascals tonight and go home with anyone in there."

"You could do the same."

"This is a job, Zee. It's professional fucking. My personal life is something else. I *do* go out to meet people and so should you."

"But this is a way to meet someone," I said.

"Are you out of your mind?"

"But I met *you*."

He stared hard at me. "Let's go to bed."

Afterwards, I propped myself up on an elbow. "Mark?"

"Don't keep calling me Mark. That's not my real name."

"It isn't?"

Smiling at me, he said, "No-o."

"You don't use your real name?"

"Zee, c'mon, smart guy, think about it. Use that brain. Of course I don't use my real name. None of the boys use their real names. Our *clients*, for God's sakes, don't even use their real names—unless they're using plastic and have to. It's all part of the fantasy name game: Mark, Brian, Shane, Butch, Jack."

"Well, what *is* your name?"

"Matthew."

"Matthew," I said musingly. "When I first saw you the other night, you didn't strike me as a Mark. The name bothered me. It didn't fit your character, but Matthew does."

"What exactly *is* my character?"

"A man with summer in his blood and winter in his eyes."

"And what is that supposed to mean?"

"I'll tell you next time, Matthew."

I said his name over to myself as I lay back down. I sighed.

"That was a big sigh there."

"I suppose."

"Do you know what time it is?"

I laughed, sighing again.

"Well, Zee, I *am* working."

"I know, I know."

He sat up in bed, stretching his arms over his head.

"Matthew?"

"Ye-es."

"Do you think . . . I mean, would you like to go out to dinner or a movie one night?"

"On duty or off duty?"

"I was hoping off duty."

"My God, Zee, are you asking me out on a *date*?"

I turned to study the expression on his face. He lay back down, facing me, and touched his nose to my nose, looking me in the eyes. "You are a crazy, strange, wonderful man."

I saw my face reflected in his eyes.

That astonished me and delighted me—to see my face in his eyes.

My face in his eyes.

The snow, the cold, the trees.

He stood up and started dressing.

"*The Sleeping Gypsy* is part painting and part pure poetry," Dr. Filburn said, shrugging the strap of his gym bag higher up on his shoulder, as we walked out of the athletic center into a mild snow-fall. "Rousseau had such fun with his paintings for being, essen-

tially, a serious man." He zipped up his navy blue parka. "And seeing so many Rousseaus all together was a thrilling experience. You
must go to the Modern before the show closes."

"What day would be good?" I asked.

"Wednesday," Matthew said, "that's usually a slow night for
me."

I was only half listening to Dr. Filburn, because my attention
had fixed itself on the confetti of snow falling in the cones of light
in the parking lot. The snowflakes tickled my cheeks and forehead,
clustered on my eyelashes. To be touched from above.

"Fine. Where and when?"

"Dupont Circle at eight o'clock. Then we can decide where to
go from there."

"The show closes at the end of April," Dr. Filburn went on,
"so you have a good month to get down there. Not only are the
Rousseaus there, but the permanent collection has some excellent
Schwitters and Duchamp."

Snow gathered on top of his bald head. With one sweep of his
hand, he brushed it off. My eyes were fixed on the outline of snow
on the tree branches, telephone wires, and fence railings. I stood in
the steady fall of snow as aliveness high-dived in my chest and
butterflied through my arms and legs. For the past three days, I had
worked long and hard and finished the most important collage I
had yet made: *Love Letters of Grandfather*.

"And, of course," he continued, "the Modern has *Still Life
with Chair Caning*, which deserves a good look every now and
then, for the simple fact that it is the first collage ever made in the
Western world. Not that it is in itself an extraordinary collage, but
the moment at which Picasso decided to add that piece of oil cloth
is worth contemplation. In thus doing so, he initiated an entirely

new art form in the twentieth century. Why is it that he decided to add it? Why that dimensional distortion? What compelled Picasso to tear that piece of oil cloth into an appropriate shape and attach it to that canvas?"

"Happenstance," I said.

"What's that?"

"Happenstance."

"Happenstance?"

"He was painting, destroying, removing traces of reality. Then he stopped and stared at the painting to see what was not there that needed to be there. What was that? What did it need? He continued to study the painting until he let his gaze drop and wander about his studio. He saw the oil cloth—*found* it—and realized that that was what the painting needed. Happenstance. The most remarkable objects are before you all the time, but you never know that until a limited vision forces you to recognize that object, to notice it, or, to be exact, to *find* it."

"Mmm," Dr. Filburn murmured, wiping more snow off the top of his head, his blue eyes bulging. "I suppose so, yes. Until you find the object that is before you all the time." He pulled at his lower lip, then abruptly wiped the top of his head again. "Well, I really must be going. I don't trust my car in this type of weather. If I had known it was going to snow, I would have brought my Jeep. Four-wheel drive, you know. So long."

With that, Dr. Filburn stepped forward and slipped. He waved his arms around like a penguin, balanced himself, and continued on his way. When he reached his car, he turned, waved, and shouted, "Happenstance!"

Falling.

I waved back at him as I walked to my car. Limitation forces the creative impulse. He's an odd one, but in a good way. A date. This summer, he's planning to show my love letters series in his Boston art gallery. A date with Matthew. Moreover, he sold every single one of my collages back in September. A date with a hustler. That was unbelievable good luck. "Not good luck," he had said to me—"Talent."

On a park bench in Dupont Circle, watching the water stream from the top of the marble fountain into the pool below, I sat excited and expectant. I sat agitated.

I am going on a date.   With Matthew.

I don't even know his last name, don't even have his telephone number—if he stands me up, I'll have to hire him again for a happy hour.

At eight o'clock, however, he paraded toward me with a frolicsome grin. Dark-brown canvas shoes, khaki pants, a blue belt, and a blue-and-white striped shirt. Relaxed and stylish. I was wearing a navy blue tee shirt and white pants.

We shook hands.

"You look great," he said. "The only question now is where to eat? Do you want to walk into Georgetown or stay here?"

"I'd rather stay here. Too hot to walk."

"Bootsie, Winkie and Miss Maud's then?"

"Fine."

Walking out of the Dupont Circle Park to P Street, I watched people watch us.

Two handsome men.

How proud I was to be with this dashingly good-looking man named Matthew.

At the restaurant, the waiter, slender and pale and exceedingly plain looking, his eyes set too close together, knew Matthew.

"Hey, Matthew, how's it going?"

"Fine, Jerry, you?"

"Working, working. A recreational man's lament."

Jerry giggled.

We ordered a carafe of white wine.

After he left the table, Matthew said, "He works for the escort service."

"Him?"

"Surprised?"

"He doesn't strike me as one of D.C.'s hottest men."

"But he has an eleven-inch cock and a malicious tongue. The best combination for verbal abuse."

"Verbal abuse?"

"To be humiliated and insulted."

"Men *pay* for that?"

"Men pay for everything."

Jerry returned with our carafe and took our dinner orders.

"Do a lot of the guys have other jobs?"

"Most do. Usually it's a part-time thing, moonlighting, in a manner of speaking. I know one guy who works as an accountant, a CPA, for the Treasury Department during the day and at night, he turns tricks. Then you have the basic high-school dropout, strung out on drugs. All types."

"Are you moonlighting?"

"No."

On the table next to a crystal vase with two white carnations, a candle flickered. My first glass of wine made me light-headed, giddy with the entire situation. I snatched a bread stick from the basket.

"So," Matthew said, "do you hire escorts every night?"

I snapped the bread stick in two. "I thought this was off duty?"

"It is, it is," he reassured me. "I meant, in *general*, do you hire escorts?"

"You were the first one I ever hired."

"And you called the service as a lark?"

"Not exactly as a lark."

As an appetizer, I had clams on the half shell. Matthew had a bowl of gazpacho.

I explained to him as well as I could my self-appointed task of exploring my sexual landscape: to create a sexual ethics. Fascinated, he asked me details about where I went, what I did, how I felt.

Jerry set baked Maryland crab with pilaf in front of me and grilled tuna in front of Matthew.

"That's remarkable, given your background," he said. "Most men fall into two categories: sexual behavior they consider contemptible but erotic or sexual behavior they consider commendable but so-so. They get trapped in reruns of one or the other because they can't harmonize the voice in their conscience with the music of their instincts; thus, they're a victim to both. What's needed is a hard inventory of your instincts, your background, and your needs to hammer out your sexual individuality. That requires danger and risk."

"Well," I said, "I've been cataloging the flora and fauna of my erotic landscape as much as possible this summer."

"And by doing that, you now have the excitement to explore other landscapes."

"Sure," I laughed, "the landscape of employment that my father mentioned last night."

He smiled. "Well, what do you think you'd like to do?"

"Something connected with history."

After we drank cups of iced cappuccino, we left the restaurant.

Matthew asked, "Would you like to come to my apartment?"

"Sure."

"But you'll have to walk into Georgetown."

"You live in Georgetown?"

He nodded.

"Well," I said, "it seems a little cooler now."

Matthew lived on the second floor of a Federal style house on 30th Street, between N Street and Dumbarton. The apartment door opened into a huge living room. One wall was a row of three large, double-hung sash windows that overlooked the street. A Miro lithograph hung over the fireplace. The apartment also had a dining room, a small kitchen, a pantry, and three bedrooms off one long hallway.

We sat down on a charcoal gray sofa.

"You work only for the escort service and manage to have an apartment like this in Georgetown?"

"I get a little help from . . . home."

"Oh, I see. But home doesn't know about the escort service?"

"No."

"How long *have* you been working there?"

"About three weeks."

"Three weeks! That's all?"

"Zee, what do you think? That I majored in Escort Service in college? There's not exactly job security or a pension plan in it."

"I honestly don't know what to think."

"Most guys last about three months, and that's it, unless you're a heavy-duty hustler."

"And what are you?"

"A dabbler."

I squinted at him.

"I'm just dabbling in it. I'm not going to be there much longer. Let's just say that I'm gathering up notes."

"Oh," I said, "so *you're* the one writing the graduate thesis, right?"

"In a manner of speaking."

"You *are* writing—"

"Not a thesis. A play."

"A play?"

He nodded.

"On hustlers?"

He smiled. "That's right, a comedy."

"A comedy on hustlers? And you thought *I* was crazy and strange."

Matthew Curtis came from a family of horse breeders in Middleberg, Virginia. He received a B.A. in Dramatic Arts from the University of Virginia and an M.F.A. in Playwriting from Johns Hopkins University. For a year, he worked as a stage manager at the Arena Stage in Washington. When that ended, he had the summer free and concocted this idea of writing a comedy on the escort service. Starting this September, he'll be working as a playwrighting consultant for the National Endowment for the Arts.

"But you didn't have to hustle to learn about it," I said.

"Who says I had the idea for the comedy *before* I started hustling?" A wry expression flitted across his face. "Besides, that's the best way I learn—from the inside, behind closed doors. So much of it's acting anyway. In some cases, sex is a minor role or not a role at all. Most of these fat, ugly, old men want companionship more than anything else. They hug you, kiss you, tell you how

handsome you are and . . . that's it. No sex. One man in Rockville
—one of the ugliest men I have ever seen—hires me to hold him
and tell him over and over 'I love you.' Nothing else happens."

"But that's so sad."

"Why?"

"Because it is."

"According to you, it is. There're many different scenes out
there. None of them any more or less important than another. You
should know that."

"But how many notes do you have to gather? How long do
you plan on doing this?"

"I can't say."

"You can't say?"

"No," he said quietly, lowering his eyes and studying his fingernails. "The entire situation intrigues me. You can't imagine the
look on a client's face when he sees me—he's so grateful to have
me. It's hard to explain."

"So you've started to do it just to do it?"

"Sometimes."

"Let me get this straight. At first, you *pretended* to be a hustler, *acting* the part of a hustler."

He nodded.

"Now, sometimes you *act* the part of a hustler and sometimes
you *are* a hustler?"

He looked hard at me and my logic and laughed uncertainly.
"No. I'm always acting."

"But you just said the whole situation intrigues you, that your
clients are so grateful to have you."

"Well, they are."

"Then you're not *necessarily* acting then, are you? You *are* the part."

"I don't think we need to continue this."

"Do you have any idea what your prospective major might be?" asked Dr. Edwin M. O'Donnell, S.J., Dean of the College of Arts and Sciences.

"We have to go one step further. I have one more question to ask you. Were you *acting* the part of a hustler or *were* you a hustler the first night you came over to my apartment?"

"History."

Matthew gazed steadily at me but did not answer.

All the next morning, I merely gazed at the collage, at the flow of the letters falling along the righthand side, tumbling, turning.

After a long moment, Matthew asked, "How is it that what I'm doing is any different than what you're doing?"

The large open space in the upper lefthand corner.

That night we became lovers.

What did I learn?

That you can fall in love with a hustler. The extraordinary reciprocity between surface and object.

My mother returned from Bangor. At noon, she walked into the barn studio with a lunch tray—tomato soup, coffee, and a ham sandwich. After we became lovers, I had to accept the fact that my lover drove around the Washington metropolitan area having sex with strangers. She stared at this new collage. "You found another bundle of love letters?"

"Yes. *Love Letters of Grandfather*."

"But not all these men are strangers, Zee," he told me one night before leaving for work. "Some are repeat clients, like you were."

She dropped the tray.

That did not console me.

That night I biked downtown to talk to Sabrina.

When she finished her set, she rustled off stage in her mint green evening gown and sat down with me. "Zee, darling, where have you been these past few weeks? You haven't gone and fallen in love, have you?"

I looked at her and burst into tears.

"Oh, no, my puppy," she said, wrapping her arms around me, "you have."

At her apartment, I paced back and forth in front of the blue-mirrored coffee table. I gesticulated and shouted.

Sabrina, curled languidly on her sofa, watched me. "Zee, darling, keep your voice down or the neighbors will think I've gotten into S&M."

"But he's with a strange man right now! Having sex and doing I don't know what!"

"Why in the world did you call that escort service in the first place?"

"Because I wanted to hire a hustler."

"Because you wanted to be in control."

"But I'm not in control now."

"You can't *ever* be in control of anyone, darling. You can only have control over yourself and you don't even have *that* right now."

"But he's out fucking some stranger!"

"Darling, what do you expect if you're involved with a hustler?"

"He's not a hustler."

"Okay, okay, a part-time hustler, an actor hustler."

"I don't know what I expected."

Sabrina laughed lightly. "Darling, you get into crazier situations than the queens I work with. Wanda had a fling with a hustler she picked up at the Wayside Café last week and ended up with three broken ribs. But what do you do? You fall in love."

"I wish *I* had three broken ribs," I said morosely.

"Darling, I wish you did too. That's easier to deal with."

"But, Sabrina," I said, sitting down on the sofa next to her, "what can I do? Every time he goes out, I climb the walls."

"How long have you known him?"

"Three weeks."

"That's not long, darling."

"Well, of course it isn't that long, but it seems like three *years*."

"Have you talked to him?"

"Well, in a way, but it's not as though I didn't know what was going on."

"You knew *just* what was going on."

"I didn't think it would make that much difference."

"Your lover being a hustler?" she said incredulously.

"It doesn't make much sense, does it?"

"It makes sense—*bizarre* sense but sense. You fell in love. When you fall in love, you fall in love and that's that. You can overcome any obstacle, solve any problem, climb any mountain, cross any sea, until you notice the toothpaste squeezed in the wrong place." She laughed and placed both hands on my shoulders. "Since you walked into this situation with your eyes wide open, you have to suppress the climbing-the-walls the best you can until *he* drops the hustling business. But *he* has to drop it of his own free will. Do *not* force the issue because he'll resent it."

"Are you sure?"

"Certainly, it's a woman's intuition, darling. When do I get to meet this hunk?"

At Georgetown the first three years, I roomed in the Old North dorm with Glen Sullivan, who had carrot-red hair, pale blue eyes, and more freckles on his face than skin.

Matthew and I saw her show the next night. He was overwhelmed by her singing—with such talent and proper management, she would have a great career.

Glen was also the most fidgety person I had ever met and had the worst taste in posters, but we got on tremendously.

When I introduced Sabrina to Matthew, she whispered to me, "Darling, what's the number of that escort service again?"

We were both history majors—nicknamed The Red and The Black—and we both swam for the swim team. My stroke was the butterfly and his was the backstroke. For our senior year, we moved off campus to rent a rowhouse in Volta Place.

That year we both came out.

Glen picked me up at the National Airport in his midnight blue BMW.

We attended Gay Awareness meetings, read *Christopher Street* and *The Washington Blade*, studied books on homosexuality, and every Saturday night went out dancing at the night clubs.

"How do you like this keen machine?" he asked. "She drives like a dream."

After graduation, Glen went to law school at NYU.

As we circled past the Lincoln Memorial, he pointed out his window at some punksters. "Look at those freaks! Fag bashers."

"What's that?"

"They go fag bashing in Dupont Circle. That's their latest thing to do, haven't you heard? They're all sickos, every last one of them."

As we drove along Constitution Avenue, Glen told me how just last week four punksters cornered a man in an alley off P Street and beat him to death with a baseball bat. We turned off Constitution and swung down a side street.

"Well, this is my humble abode," he said, opening the front door to his Capitol Hill apartment—all chrome and mirror, glass, and bird-of-paradise colors. "How do you like it? $750 a month, a super steal for this location."

Mustering up rental enthusiasm, I said, "That is a steal."

"You can use that closet in the hall for shirts and whatnot. You sleep on *la* sofa, there, and the sheets are in that bottom drawer." He turned on his stereo and asked me, "Don't you just *love* Madonna's new look?"

"Excuse me?"

"Madonna's new look, Zee. Don't tell me MTV doesn't exist in Maine?" He handed me an album cover with Madonna, in profile, her hair bleached white. "Isn't that fabulous? And you should see the hunk in her 'Papa Don't Preach' video. Utterly gorgeous. I sit and drool in front of the TV."

I stared at Glen. The same red hair, though cut short and styled. The same face, though fuller. The same jumpy disposition, though peevish and effeminate. At least the freckles haven't changed. This was not my college roommate. This was not even what my college roommate could *not* have become.

"Zee, honey, why don't we go grab a bite to eat at the American Café—that's where *everyone* goes on Thursday nights. Then we go dancing at Badlands. Badlands is the place to go on Thursday. Lost and Found on Friday. Tracks on Saturday. Lost and Found again for Sunday tea."

Sabrina said not to force the issue, so I didn't force the issue.

"Badlands is the place to go on Thursday," I repeated in a monotone.

Hours were turned upside down.

I slept during the day and stayed up all night—a vampire life.

"That's right, the only place. Now freshen up a bit and we'll get going."

"I'd like to get a bite to eat, but I don't think I want to go dancing at Badlands."

A displaced vampire because I spent most of my time at Matthew's apartment, returning to mine only for more clothes or a book.

Glen stared at me, disbelief stamped on his face. "But it's a Thursday night!"

At six in the morning, Matthew staggered through the door. He searched through his pubic hair for lice, then jumped in the shower.

He slept until two in the afternoon, climbed out on the rooftop with a cup of iced coffee to sunbathe, then disappeared into his study to write for the rest of the day until dinner. After dinner, he read until Denny called him.

I followed the same pattern.

I helped him search his pubic hair for lice.

I slept until two in the afternoon. Usually, I woke first, made the coffee, and woke Matthew by grabbing his big toe and shaking it.

I climbed out on the roof to sunbathe.

After sunbathing, we fucked.

I disappeared on my bike when he disappeared into his study. I biked thirty or forty miles an afternoon until dinner. We always dined out—eating our way through every Georgetown restaurant.

I sat with him on the sofa and read until that telephone rang disturbingly for "Mark."

The sound of the ice makes mysterious sounds when you try to sleep: grinding, groaning, creaking.

When he left for work, I biked again through the Washington streets until my head throbbed and my legs ached. Back at the apartment, I read until dawn until Matthew staggered through the door.

Saturday night. Matthew emerged from the bedroom dressed in work boots, torn dungarees, a dirty white tee shirt, and a yellow hard hat. One closet was crammed with various hats and shirts and shoes for different fantasies.

"This is for that seedy fat man in Arlington, isn't it?" I asked.

"Seedy fat men need love, too," he said flippantly.

I glared at him.

Opening the front door, he said, "See you Sunday morning. If Denny calls, tell him I've gone to Mr. Jacobson's place."

The door shut.

I threw *The New Yorker* down on the floor and walked aimlessly from room to room for fifteen minutes.

Then I went for a bike ride.

The night was cool, so I wore my white windbreaker and remembered that the last time I had worn it was the night I had met Sabrina.

Saturday night traffic and crowds muddled the streets and sidewalks.

"Hey, watch out!" an old man crossing the street shouted at me as I zipped past him, close to him, working my way up Wisconsin Avenue.

At Q Street, I darted past a red Mercedes sedan, cutting across the intersection in front of it. The car slammed on its brakes and blared its horn.

I pumped hard down Q Street into Dupont Circle, swung past the Metro station, and climbed the hill. At the civil war monument of General George Brinton McClelland, I turned around, stopped at the red light, and fixed my eyes on Connecticut Avenue—the cars and the string of traffic lights.

I was at the top of the steepest part of Connecticut Avenue.

The street sloped down sharply,

dipped underground at the Dupont Circle Park,

and continued a steady decline until K Street.

Once you go,   you go, zipping along at thirty or forty miles per hour.

If you hit the right speed, you can fly through green lights at every single intersection until you make K Street.

That was a biking game some friends of mine used to play.

I had never done that before, but one friend of mine said that he had done it twice.

The traffic light turned green and I set off, shifting into tenth gear, bending down parallel to the cross bar, gripping my hands on the dropped handlebar.

I squinted into the night and pedaled as hard as I could, imagining myself already at the final traffic light on K Street.

I sailed down Connecticut Avenue, past Florida Avenue and R Street, Q Street, dipped into the tunnel under the Dupont Circle Park, and cannonballed out the other side past O Street and N Street. I saw K Street in the distance when the traffic light at M Street turned yellow. I can just make it, make it, faster.

A black car changed lanes.

I saw the white lane dividers

on the street,   sudden hyphenations
of wheels on top of
headlights,   headlights
bright with thumps of yellow, red, and green lights,
lights with shoulders and arms and blackness.

When I opened my eyes, I winced. My shoulder hollered.
The back of my head doubled over. I tried to sit up, but Matthew
held me down.

"Lie still, big guy," he said firmly.

I had a blurry vision of Matthew and whiteness and I thought
I heard Sabrina whispering before my eyelids dropped shut.

I heard Sabrina singing when I opened my eyes the
next time.

I turned my head slightly and saw a yellow hard hat on a
table.

Matthew stood next to the table.

He suddenly started clapping.   Then I heard more clapping.

"What's going on?" I asked hoarsely.

Matthew turned to me and came over to my side. He motioned in the air. The clapping subsided as Sabrina, wearing a tangerine gown, appeared at the foot of my bed.

"Where am I?"

"The emergency room, big guy," Matthew said. "You took a
terrific tumble on your bike, right in the middle of Connecticut Avenue."

"Oww."

"Don't sit up, darling," Sabrina said. "You have a mild concussion."

"You've got to wear a helmet," Matthew said, "if you're going to bike like a mad man."

"Did I break any bones?"

"Not any arms or legs," Matthew said, "but they still have to x-ray your shoulder."

"How did *you* get here?" I asked him.

"All you had was Sabrina's card zipped in the pocket of your windbreaker, so the hospital called her."

"And, darling, I was right in the middle of my set when Eddie called me off stage to say the GW Emergency Room was on the line. When the woman said it was a bicycle accident, I ran screaming into the street to hail a cab. I called the escort service when I got here. I must say the nurses and doctors were surprised when *I* walked in."

"And when I called in to the escort service," Matthew continued, "Denny told me what had happened. I drove over as fast as I could and rushed in here without even taking off my hard hat."

Sabrina laughed lightly. "The nurses couldn't keep their eyes off him."

"And the doctors couldn't keep their eyes off Sabrina."

Matthew and Sabrina laughed.

"We've been here ever since," Matthew said, "waiting for you to wake up."

"One of the nurses recognized me from the club and before I knew it, they had a portable stereo playing and I was singing songs."

Then it hit me that he was *here*, with me, and Sabrina, too. I started to cry.

Matthew stroked my head and said that I would be all right, that a mild concussion isn't all that bad. Sabrina patted my hand.

My shoulder wasn't broken.

The doctor explained, however, that I had completely flipped

over, smacked the car's trunk with my back, bounced off, and hit
the street hard with my right shoulder before I pitched into uncon-
sciousness. He said it was sheer luck that my shoulder took the
full impact of the fall and not my head, or I might have been sleeping for a good long while. He released me with a prescription for
Tylenol III, complete rest for the week, and an emphasis upon the
importance of helmets and bicycle paths.

My right arm was tied up in a sling. My body ached, especially
my shoulder. As Matthew and Sabrina helped me through the doors
of the emergency room, I said, "But where's my bicycle?"

"You'll see," Matthew said.

Outside he pointed to a tree. Against it was a crumpled heap
of bike—a twisted frame, no rear tire, and handlebars that dangled.

In January 1899, at midnight, Peary and his expedition
reached Fort Conger in northern Ellesmere Island. It had been a
difficult march in the dead of winter, stormy and bitterly cold, tem-
peratures as low as minus 63 degrees Fahrenheit.

"A pick-up truck ran over it after you flipped over on the car.
The car didn't even stop, but the guy driving the truck stopped and
called the ambulance. He brought your bike here for you."

"Oh, well, so much for that bicycle," I said.

Henson had wanted to wait until spring, but Otto Svedrup, a
Norwegian explorer, was marching northward. Peary did not want
any other explorer to get latitudinally one-up on him, so he
marched in midwinter moonlight hundreds of miles sledging supplies.

Matthew picked it up and threw it in a dumpster. His red con-
vertible Karmen Ghia was parked on the street. He opened the
door for me and helped me in. Sabrina sat up in back, like a queen
on a parade float, and warbled, "What a darling car this is."

Finally, they stumbled through the dilapidated door of Fort Conger and started fires in the stoves. At that point, Peary, suspicious of a wooden feeling in his right foot, asked Henson to remove his kamiks (seal skin boots) and rabbit skin undershoes. Henson inserted the blade of his knife under the top of the kamiks, sliced through the skins, and pulled them off.

Peary's legs were a bloodless white up to his knees.

When Henson ripped off an undershoe, two or three toes snapped off at the first joint, clinging to the hide.

His feet were frosted.

All the toes, except the little ones, had to be amputated. This mutilation was a serious handicap since walking, especially with snowshoes, required effective use of the toes.

When my father saw the collage, he gulped at the air as though he had been punched in the gut. He clenched his hands into fists. His eyes were spinning.

"I remember few more grim and desolate scenes than the environs of Fort Conger as I took them in while being lashed to my sledge, a helpless cripple, on the bitterly cold February morning when I left the fort to return to the ship *Windward*."

"How can you have done this?" His voice erupted into this high-pitched shriek. "How can you have done this to my father's letters?"

I stared at him and then at the collage.

Another defeat, another setback. But Peary refused to despair. On the wall of the old cabin, he wrote the line from Seneca that had long been his guiding motto: *Inveniam viam aut faciam.* "I shall find a way or make one."

"You destroyed them!"

"I haven't," I said quietly.

"You haven't?"

"No, Papa. I preserved them. Artistically."

My father held the sides of his head. "My God my God, don't you know the value of those letters?"

"Yes."

"And you did *this*?" He shook a fist wildly at the collage. "You did this to my father's love letters?" Again, he gestured at the collage. "This is Gregor Matejcic of Croatia. My father. And you have destroyed his letters."

"I recreated them."

"Recreated, Christ!" he bellowed. "Destroyed! It's not just paper and ink you're toying with! Those letters are *words, intimate* words, *tender* words you obviously cannot understand. You . . . what do you know about love? You . . . you're. . . ."

What do you say to

"Gay, Papa."

a young man dying?

"You know nothing about love! Nothing!" He stared contemptuously at the collage and hissed, "And this perversity proves it."

For the next week, Matthew took care of me. He never left the apartment except to go to buy groceries or the *Washington Post.* He spent most of the day working on his comedy.

My father quarreled violently with my mother, said he wanted everything cleared out of the barn, and refused to talk to me.

Denny called three or four times a day and begged Matthew to work, but he refused each time. Finally, he quit. He had had enough.

What do you know about love?

"Seven weeks working for an escort service is seven

weeks too long," he said.

"Are you sure?"

The next morning a strong, tight wind gripped the sides of the barn and the narrow planks of wood gasped. I could not work. My fingers were numb.

"For God's sake, I don't know how you put up with it, now that I've had the time to think about it."

A feeble smile tightened my face.

I heard the door to the ell open.

At the end of August, I moved into Matthew's apartment. "Zee?"

I did not answer, did not move, did not turn my head.

"Zee?" my mother called again.

I sat slumped in a chair, grinding my teeth, staring vacantly into space, holding a scrap of white paper.

A ragged circle.   My thumb jerked back and forth over the grainy surface as though searching for a thumb print.

A single lamp glowed on the picnic table.

The Quartz space heater steadily thrummed its orange heat into the air.

The wind slapped the barn again and again the planks gasped.

"Zee?" she called again loudly. She stepped past the edge of a canvas looking toward the dim light. "Are you—"

She stopped. Behind me stood *Love Letters of Grandfather*.

She pulled the front of her cardigan together, pushed a strand of hair behind her ear, and said softly, "Zee."

I said nothing.

"Would you like some coffee?"

I turned to her, as a bone snapped in my neck.   I shook my head, no.

"Some hot cocoa?"

I closed my eyes and shook my head, once, no.

"Are you sure?"

I inhaled deeply, opened my eyes, and looked at her.

        "He never should have

She dropped her eyes to the collar of my flannel shirt.

        said that to me."

"He had no right to insult me that way. He had no right to say that. Never. Not even so much what he said but the tone of his voice—the way he *shouted.*"

She dropped her eyes farther to the scrap of paper in my hand and said quietly, "Those letters meant a great deal to him."

"And they don't mean anything to me?" I demanded, my voice rising. "They have no meaning for *me*?"

I saw her eyes film with tears.

"Have you ever thought or has *he* ever thought that those letters might mean *more* to me than to him?"

"Perhaps . . . perhaps, I should never. . . ."

"Mother, you did nothing wrong."

"But none of this would have happened and . . . and. . . ."

She pressed her lips together into a firm line. She couldn't speak. She turned from me and stared at the collage.

A lead is a lane of black sea water, a fracture in the ice field, caused by the pressure of winds and tides against the ice.

"What am I supposed to do about my studio?"

She shook her head.

Leads are the most unpredictable and dangerous aspect of Arctic exploration and often the sole reason for failed expeditions because a lead stops movement dead.

"Maybe if I go away for a little while, that would help."

A lead opens without warning, following no apparent rule or law of action.

"Where would you go?"

"Anywhere."

For a week, I sat in my studio and did nothing. I couldn't work. That restless energy had disappeared. I decided to return to Washington and called Glen to see if I could stay with him, just for a week or two.

The East Wing of the National Gallery of Art.

Before Peary could continue his march north, he had to wait until the ice floes floated together again or until that open section of the sea froze enough to support the weight of dogs, sledge, and man.

The light questioned my face.

Merzhaus.

The Calder mobile walked over me.

To Rothko.

> Those luminous, quiet rectangles
>
> floating in a landscaped endlessness.

I sat down.

I sat down   to sit.

To marvel at those rectangles.

But a dull ache rose from the polished wood floor. Tired, blunted, stupid. I had lost all interest in the National Archives, did not care if I ever saw Matthew again, and no longer cared to pander to my father's talk about job security and salary and GS level. The city itself oppressed me.

Collage.

That is what I want. I need time. I need space and size. I need freedom.

Matthew, the National Archives, my father, the city all leagued against me. I fixed each one in each corner of the upper rectangle of the Rothko painting and in the center of the lower rectangle fixed myself. That much I carry. Too much.

A husky, a polar bear, an Eskimo child: the transformation of the spirit.

The East Wing of the National Gallery of Art.

I sat down in front of the Rothko.

Washington, Matthew, and the National Archives had all disappeared—except my father. My father now filled the entire upper rectangle, crushing me. In two weeks, Dr. Filburn would be showing my love-letters series in Boston; *Love Letters of Grandfather*, however, was not for sale. Dr. Filburn said the restricted subject matter and the limited materials liberated a subtle and dynamic quality not present in my earlier work. He expected good publicity and, most important, good sales.

A husky, harnessed to a sledge, obediently accepts the heaviest load it can carry before it sets out for the desert waste of arctic ice. All the supplies of the heart and mind. All the toilsome questions of journey. All the burdens of past and present, future and lost.

What do you say to a young man dying?

What does the spirit know or not know?

The voices of need. Then the husky in the desolate frigidity changes into the polar bear—the beast of whiteness. The claws of antipodes. The white beast roars above the voices of need and tears into the supplies and questions and mangles the burdens. What values are these in the waste of ice? Then the final change into the Eskimo child. The beginning of the beginning and the end of the end. To become.

It is only honest men or scoundrels who can find an escape from any situation. Who said that? Where did I read that? Or hear that?

I honked my horn and braked hard as a yellow sports car swerved in front of me on I-95 North.

"Fool!" I shouted. The U-Haul trailer, jammed with all my belongings, bounced and lurched behind my car.

Miss Doin sat at her desk, surprised, disconcerted, disappointed, and said, "Zee, you are twenty-six years old, which is very very young, and now head of Special Collections. That is quite an achievement. Are you sure you want to resign?"

Matthew sat at the kitchen table, crying, saying over and over, "But I love you, Zee." I stood leaning against the counter, staring dry-eyed into the sink, and felt cold sadness drift into my face.

My father said sternly, "What are you telling me? That you're leaving the National Archives to make collages? Have you lost all sense of reason?"

Is this the correct decision?

Should I have done otherwise?

But that restless and intense curiosity to create marched over any doubts I had.

With two suitcases and a knapsack, I boarded a plane at the Bangor International Airport. Ragged clumps of cloud, the color of oysters and some the shape of oysters, slid rapidly overhead, low in the sky. My eyes were leaden, my hands were cold, and my face was blank.

In Maine I would make collages. In Maine I would explore the landscape of my imagination with boldness, consciousness, and attention. My eyes, bright with anticipation and apprehension, peered at a world of color, shape, surface, and texture.

I stared dully out the window at the clouds, a flat gray expanse.

Idly I wondered how well Glen and I would get along after so many years. At least I have a place to stay. I wish Sabrina were still in town. She had moved back to New York City three years ago. I'll stop in at the National Archives to say hello to everyone. But do I want to see Matthew? No.   Not yet.

With two suitcases and a knapsack, I bordered a plane at the National Airport on a hot, hazy, June afternoon. My eyes were clear with determination, my hands were moist, and my face was shining.

I fell asleep, burdened with *Love Letters of Grandfather*, and didn't wake until the plane touched down at the National Airport.

Out the window, I watched the rolling white fields of clouds.

I tried to rest, but couldn't, too excited by the collage I held in my mind. The flight seemed interminably long.

It must be a perfect unity—asymmetrical symmetry.

The letters together.

The landing lights came on, and I could see the glittering Atlantic Ocean and the deep dark green of the Maine coastline. This will be affirmation. The plane touched down at the Bangor International Airport.

The worst obstacles Peary encountered in his quest for the North Pole were the natural conditions of the Arctic. Jagged and mountainous ice over which he had to travel with his heavily loaded sledge. The often terrific wind slammed into him with the impact of a wall of water, against which he had to march. The leads that he somehow had to cross and recross. And the intense cold.

Affirmation of male love.

What do you say to a young man dying?

So life together commenced.

What do you know about love?

I always woke first, showered, and, toweling my hair dry, woke Matthew by grabbing his big toe and shaking it until he woke up and smiled at me.

We walked to Foggy Bottom and rode the Metro downtown—he to the NEA, I to the National Archives.

Dinner: we flip-flopped preparing dinners with eating out at restaurants.

An occasional movie, reading, dancing on Saturday nights, and attending plays since part of Matthew's job at the NEA encompassed seeing various stage companies and their productions.

I stopped cigarette smoking and started swimming again, three or four times a week at the Georgetown University pool.

Whenever I flew home to Maine to visit my parents, I always wrote Matthew long and detailed letters describing my weekends.

During that first year together, Matthew also worked evenings and weekends on his play.

In the spring of 1981, Matthew finally finished his comedy on the escort service and submitted it to various stage companies in the Washington metropolitan area. Within three weeks, the Capitol Playhouse, a small local theater in Adams Morgan, expressed an interest in it. The theater did a reading during the summer and staged a production in the fall.

On opening night, Matthew, Sabrina, and I sat together.

The response was magnificent—the audience chuckled and laughed and clapped.

Two weeks later, a representative from Arena Stage, one of

the most prestigious stage companies in Washington, saw a production and also expressed an interest in it.

The first opportunity for a reading, however, would be the summer of 1982.

"Do you realize what this means?" Matthew said.

A longer run, a far better group of actors, greater publicity— he was on the proverbial way.

I sent him a bouquet of balloons at work with a message congratulating him and telling him how much I loved him.

We dined at Le Pavillon, a nouvelle French cuisine restaurant in Dupont Circle and the most expensive restaurant in town. I tasted *foie gras* for the first time. I sat watching Matthew and felt happiness strapped to my back.

Then in May 1982 *The New York Times* published a major article on "New Homosexual Disorder."

By the summer of 1982, Arena Stage explained to Matthew that they couldn't consider producing such a play about gay sexual antics, given the circumstances of this deadly new disease. Later, possibly, when more is known.

Matthew had anticipated their reaction, knowing that a comedy about sex was out of place when gay civil rights groups were fighting for more federal funding to investigate this disease no one knew anything about.

His comedy *Dialing for Pleasures* came to an abrupt stop.

After he talked to the director at Arena Stage, he got drunk that night. I had never seen him drink like that before. He sat in the living room, drinking vodka on the rocks, the bottle in front of him with a bucket of ice.

I stood by an armchair. "So what do you plan

He stared at me with contempt.

to do?"

"I plan," he said slurringly, "to get blind drunk."

"I meant beyond tonight."

"How the fuck am I supposed to know? Tomorrow night, I'll try whiskey. The next, I'll try rum. There. I have two more nights planned."

I studied my fingernails.

"Then I'll take a Qualuude."

"You could start writing a new play," I suggested.

"Then after that, I'll drop acid."

I left the room.

243 persons with AIDS had died by the fall of 1982.

Miss Doin was not only startled to see me but visibly excited. "Zee, I want to show you something."

During 1983, Matthew hardly wrote at all.

She lead me through the building, past where my old office used to be, and stopped at the end of the hall in front of a large oil painting encased in a gaudy, gold, baroque picture frame.

He went to work, attended plays, continued business socializing. He even bought a small Sony TV and started watching television programs. He was morose and listless. He lost weight.

"That," she pronounced, "is Peary."

A representational portrait. I leaned forward to read the title of the picture on a small brass plate centered in the bottom half of the frame: *The Arctic Explorer*.

"Painted by N.C. Wyeth," she explained, "Andrew Wyeth's father."

I gazed at Peary, who was life-size and dressed in a caribou Eskimo suit.

Against a gray-white background, he stood on a pair of snow-shoes with his arms stiff at his sides. A grim face, a determined expression, resolute eyes. I smiled at the handlebar mustache above his thin lips and imagined him harmonizing "Old Man River" in a barbershop quartet instead of racing a dog sled across the frozen Arctic Sea to become the first man ever to stand on the North Pole. Irreverently, I glanced at his crotch and thought of that other handlebar mustache in The Falcon so many years ago.

"It's quite an impressive painting, don't you think?" Miss Doin asked.

I nodded vaguely.

"This painting was also part of what we acquired from the National Geographic Society. It arrived shortly after you left."

She pulled out a set of keys, unlocked the door to the office at the end of the hall, and held the door open. "If you please."

When I entered the room, I saw all seventeen boxes marked with black letters.

NGS   PEARY   CONFIDENTIAL

Little else was in the room except a desk and chair.

Miss Doin stood at the door, her arms folded over her chest.

"Zee, could we have a serious talk?"

It turned out that the only persons with adequate knowledge of the National Archives Special Collections Division were herself, Mr. Potter, Mrs. Stillwater, and me. Miss Doin herself could not possibly take the time to go through this material, and Mr. Potter and Mrs. Stillwater were involved in projects that could not be interrupted. It had been a severe blow to her, Miss Doin had to admit, when I resigned last year just as the Peary material arrived because she had hoped I would be the one to sift through all the material and prepare it for Special Collections.

By the spring of 1984, I managed to advance to the highest
level as Head of Special Collections in Miss Doin's department—
a result of my conscientious and competent manner as well as the
unexpected heart attack of Mr. Coates, the previous head. It was
quite extraordinary to have such a young man in such a position of
responsibility, but Miss Doin vouched for my knowledge, reliabil-
ity, and competence; she further emphasized that time would be
wasted trying to find another candidate and training him or her
when I had worked so closely with Mr. Coates for two years.

For weeks now, she has been evading Mr. Wilson, the lawyer
for the Peary family, who had been inquiring about the status of
the Peary Papers. Since I was in Washington for an undetermined
period of time, would I possibly consider preparing and cataloging
the Peary material?

By the spring of 1984, I had also managed to advance to a position of dullness and enervation, constraint and restriction, routine
and monotony.

My job had started to bore me.

"How long would this take?" I asked.

"I can't say, Zee. I don't know what those boxes contain. But
with your knowledge and experience, I doubt that it would take
more than three months."

"Three months."

"And, of course, you would receive a generous compensa-
tion."

By the spring of 1984, AIDS had also advanced to national attention and fatal concern—young men were dying and dying fast.

By the spring of 1984, Matthew and I had been lovers for
three and half years.

Routine, however, defined the relationship: routine conversation, routine dining out, routine lovemaking. The dull, blunted habit of love.

Matthew and I had a quarrel—over going to the movies. I didn't want to go.

"So what do you want to do?" he asked.

By the spring of 1984, my body yearned for change and challenge and danger as it had in the summer of 1980. Perhaps I could have thrown myself into a love affair, but AIDS eliminated any enthusiasm for that type of recklessness. How could I be reckless?

"I don't want to go to the movies."

"No, you don't want to go to the movies or out to a concert or a play or out dancing. All you want to do is hole yourself up in that back room and paste your colored papers together."

I regarded him impassively as his face turned gray with anger.

"When was the last time we went out to a movie together?" he asked.

"Not too long ago."

Miss Doin upbraided me for not having the archives messengers prepared to accept the boxes from the National Geographic Society for the transaction of the Peary materials that spring of 1985.

He bit his lower lip. "Six weeks ago, Zee. I counted. That was the last time we did something. Don't you think we should spend more time together?"

"Do you think so?" I asked coldly.

"Do you know how embarrassed I was to have to ask those men to wait outside until I found the proper transfer documents?"

I said I could imagine.

He stared at me as sadness drifted into his eyes.

"And well you should, Zee. This is one of the most important acquisitions we have had in the past ten years and on the morning of its arrival, we were unprepared!" Miss Doin could not mask her chagrin, disappointment, and anger. "You should view the Peary material as one of the most important historical materials you'll ever prepare for Special Collections. This is a rare opportunity, young man."

I said that I agreed with her and lied about having marked the wrong day on my calender.

"That is quite unlike you, Zee."

There is so much that is quite unlike me, Miss Doin.

The messengers lugged box upon box into my office.

Seventeen boxes in all.

I still couldn't believe there had been this much material forgotten in a basement, but I couldn't cope with it at the moment and told my secretary that I had a terrific headache and would be going home for the rest of the afternoon.

Diligently I worked through March and April and most of May: organizing, classifying, writing short summaries describing contents, having material prepared for microfilming, researching dates and persons. Seven of the boxes contained books from Peary's personal library that required simple notation of the titles and authors and which books were heavily annotated.

I didn't go home to Georgetown.

I went to the East Wing of the National Gallery of Art.

At the beginning of May, Miss Doin introduced me to Dr. Emmet Ender, a polar explorer and professor of astronomy at Harvard University.

He had been hired by the National Geographic Society and the Peary family to conduct research in the National Archives. A recent television docudrama had stirred up the old Cook/Peary controversy by claiming that Dr. Frederick A. Cook had discovered the North Pole first. The Peary family requested that a competent scientist examine all pertinent records and materials preserved in the National Archives and release his findings to defend Peary's claim to the North Pole.

Dr. Ender was a man in his mid-fifties, short, impeccably dressed, imperious green eyes, with a distinct Massachusetts accent, but the very tip of his nose was missing—frostbite on his first polar expedition in 1961.

Miss Doin explained that Dr. Ender was first going to examine all the documents, letters, records, scientific journals, and findings that were already preserved in the National Archives before examining all the new material I was working on. Since I was most familiar with the Peary Papers at this point, she assigned me to assist Dr. Ender.

Dr. Ender noticed the photograph of Peary tacked on my bulletin board. He stepped over to inspect it. "His 1906 expedition?"

"No," I said, "that photo was taken on the *Roosevelt* after he returned from the North Pole."

"Hmm," he muttered, not turning around. "Peary is one of my heroes."

"He had a heroic stature."

"But we must," he said, turning to face me, "be objective."

Miss Doin glanced uneasily at me.

In 1909 Peary and Henson had sailed out of New York Harbor on the ship *Roosevelt*, heading north for Cape Sheridan of Ellesmere Island, where they set off on their historic journey. Peary had over two hundred pieces of music in his collection, but the strains of *Faust* rolled out over the Arctic Ocean more often than any other.

The next morning I called work and said I wouldn't be in. I went to the National Institute of Health in Bethesda, Maryland.

"What I most want you to do now is to keep your eyes open for all papers marked with figures or computation," Dr. Ender said in a business-like manner. "That is most what I need at this point."

On the third floor, I followed the nurse into a room where Matthew lay with tubes hooked up to his nostrils, his arms, and his penis.

She stopped at the foot of the hospital bed, and I stopped beside her.

"Matthew," she said gently.

I stood rigid, my hands lightly touching the aluminum rails fencing him in.

I stared straight into his gray, ravaged face.

"Matthew," she called again gently.

When he didn't respond, she lifted the clipboard attached to the end of the bed and studied it.

"He should be awake now. Perhaps if you wait a little while, he'll wake up. If he does, have him drink a little water before he tries to talk. The AZT dehydrates him."

I nodded as I glanced at the plastic cup and the bent straw. The nurse then left us alone.

Unblinkingly, I stared at my former lover.

Is this possible?   In a year?

I shifted my weight from one foot   to the other.

All of a sudden, my eyes itched and I blinked a few times.

I ran my fingers through my hair, tucking it behind my ears. I clamped my hand over my chin and mouth. Something inside my face was cracking and pulling apart as I squeezed my eyes shut, taking a jagged breath through my nose. I rubbed my hand over my face.

"Matthew," I whispered.

I grabbed his big toe and shook it.

"Matthew, time to wake up."

Time to wake up from this nightmare.

Wake up and walk out and laugh and cry.

Take off that Halloween costume,

    but he lay there,

unmoving,

        an abandoned piece of battered, sleeping flesh.

"And I've sold five collages," I went on quietly, "my big ones, and there's another exhibition of my work going on right now. I was so productive this past year until I had a blow-up with my father."

Queasiness spiraled up my chest and suddenly I was frightened.

I was being taken somewhere I didn't want to go.

My legs quaked as I sat down in a chair at the head of the bed.

I bent my head down, staring at the linoleum floor. My brain lurched. I held my head in my hands.

Peary considered a season spent in the arctic a great test of character. He claimed that he knew a man better after six months in the frozen wilderness than after a lifetime in the frenetic cities.

Then I looked up. The nurse stood in the doorway with a doctor.

"Yes," I said, sitting up straight in the chair.

        Peary didn't know what to call it that was in the lonely white spaces that forced a man to confront himself, but that self-confrontation happened. If a man was a man, then the man emerged; if the man was a coward, then the coward started to howl.

"Mr. Matejcic?" Dr. Thornton said.

"Yes."

"If you don't mind, I'd like to have a word with you in my office."

2) Anonymous sex.

What do you say to a young man dying?

What is anonymous sex?

Peary devoted 32 years of his life trying to reach the North Pole. When he finally got there, he spent 30 hours on the top of the world.

Having sex with a stranger, someone you don't know and someone you will never see again.

In many instances, anonymous sex overlaps with other sexual practices on a variety of levels.

You meet a man in a bar, chit-chat, go to his apartment or hotel room, pass the night in heaps and stacks of sexual confrontation, and confess the desire to meet again through the ritualistic exchange of telephone numbers—that is the *least* of anonymity, the classic one-night stand; the *most* of anonymity, the classic anonymous encounter, is ten minutes, fifteen minutes, half an hour at the most, with a man in a public place where discovery—and arrest— is possible.

This element of danger and risk, exposure and humiliation, heightens the intensity of the sexual contact.

You do not talk.

This type of sexual confrontation happens in parks, at beaches, in the back row of movie theaters, in rest stops on highways, and public bathrooms.

Megan Park, a public park in Georgetown, is a notorious park where gay men congregate at all hours for anonymous sexual encounters.

After the bars and clubs close on a Friday or Saturday night, those who did not meet someone for the night spill over to Megan Park for one last attempt at sex.

From two o'clock in the morning until daybreak, the park swarms with gay men.

One night at three o'clock in the morning, I cruised down P Street toward the park.

Just before I reached it, a police cruiser drove slowly past me and set my heart winding tightly in my chest.

When I reached the entrance to the park, I had my set of rules intact (learned from the porno theater)—the least stimulus produces the greatest response.

I entered Megan Park. Tall, slender ginkgo trees lined the tarmac path that lead into the park. Crepe myrtles, maples, sycamores, and the blunted shapes of chestnut trees crowded the dark landscape.

The summer air was cool, moist, and misty that early in the morning.

Keys dropped from the maples and spun to the ground.

Lamplights shadowed the extensive lawn.

I saw men moving along the edges.

One man, smoking a cigarette, scuffled past me. I watched the red tip of his cigarette disappear down a dirt path into the woods.

I followed the red tip.

Dark trees.

I stumbled over a root.

I saw figures shadowed behind tree trunks.

Early morning sounds were distinct and eerie.

I smelled cigarette smoke, green leaves, and earth.

Men stood, stared, shuffled, wandered among the dark trees.

I leaned against a sycamore tree and lit a cigarette.

An American chestnut squatted nearby, its branches sprouting like a beard from the base of a long-dead tree. Its branches drooped with long, white, fuzzy catkins. Chestnuts had been wiped out by the chestnut blight in 1904, but recently, suddenly, new growth had burst forth from the dead trunks.

A young black man ambled past me.   We were alone.

I tossed my cigarette to the ground and crushed it out.

I glanced at my wristwatch.

This young black man was tall and muscle-thick, with coffee-colored skin.

The moonlight drenched the trees in silver and pearl.

When I tossed my cigarette down, as though it were a gesture of approach, he walked over to me and stopped and stared down the path.

His hand brushed my crotch.

My heart tightened, but I made no movement and said nothing.

His hand rubbed my crotch. He then stared at me, sexual agitation painted on his face.

He walked farther into the woods, past the beard-like chestnut tree.

I followed.

Not far from the chestnut tree, he stopped and leaned against a maple.

I stood in front of him.

He pulled me into him and kissed me on the mouth, his

tongue exploring.

He pulled out a bottle of poppers and held it under my nose.

My heart wound itself into a tight prick of nothingness as lightningthundered through my brain.

I kissed him back and swooned into the eroticism.

Tightly I held him as I rubbed his crotch.

We pulled our tank tops up around our necks and pulled down our jeans.

There I stood in Megan Park with my jeans around my ankles and my shirt around my neck, kissing and fondling and sucking and licking this perfect stranger until we both came.

He pulled up his jeans, pulled down his shirt, and   left.

Breathing heavily, I stood leaning against the tree trunk and smelled the unmistakable odor of semen.

Haze obscured the sun. Dull, leaden light saturated the sky. This light fell on the white surface of the ice and made it impossible to see for any considerable distance. The atmosphere turned unreal in this ghastly and shadowless gray luminosity that destroyed all relief.

I sniffed again. That sharp, sarcastic smell—Chlorox and bitters. I examined myself but I was clean.

The pungent odor, however, grew stronger as I neared the beardlike chestnut tree. I sniffed its branches. The scent of the catkin, the flower of this tree, was the smell of semen—that strong, healthy, erotic odor of sex. I looked at my wristwatch again.

All afternoon I waited for Matthew to wake up, but he never did. I said good-bye to him, my face jumbled with disbelief.

What did I learn?

It is possible to have a full sexual experience in sixteen minutes, and the catkin of a chestnut tree smells like semen.

As I marched down the corridor, I gazed straight ahead as though peering into that unreal light that blends sky, horizon, and ice into one flat gray plane, detached from the ordinary world.

I rode the Metro to Dupont Circle.

I walked home abstracted.

By the time I stopped in front of the McKinnon townhouse, the humid twilight had pasted my white cotton shirt to my back.

My gaze climbed all three stories to study the Hopper-like yellow light vibrating in every window.   Figures jumped and twisted in the bay window.

I focused on the profusion of wisteria blossoms that sur-rounded the front door—triangulate clumps of dangling purple. I could smell the fragrance of the high-climbing vine, a blend of honey, lilac, and Kool-aid.

I could almost taste the sweet fragrance as my mind swirled with purple shapes. What Bonnard could have done with that wisteria vine.

"Lions and punksters and bears, oh my!"

Three teenage girls, one black and two white, all dressed in black jeans and black turtlenecks with the sleeves ripped off, their arms interlaced, skipped singing down the center of the street to-ward me.

"Lions and punksters and bears, oh my!"

They skipped past me, skipped up the front sidewalk to the front door, and pounded simultaneously with their fists.

The door opened and released a burst of unrecognizable mu-sic.

The girls skipped inside.

The door slammed shut.

What's going on? Where's Mrs. McKinnon?

I walked up the front sidewalk and just as I placed my hand on the doorknob, the front door jerked open. A bulky football-player of a boy hurtled through the doorway, slammed into me, and knocked me down.

"Hey, dude,

From the sidewalk I gaped up at a blurry, pock-marked face and five green spikes.you okay?" Tiny discs of purple and green light "Hey, dude,jumped at the corners of my eyes.
you okay?"

"Jabberwocky, what the . . . Zee! Jesus, Zee, you okay? What the hell happened?"

"You know this dude?"

"He lives here, you big fuck!"

"But he's not even dressed

I saw the single, solitary, platinum-blond spike.   in black."

"Unicorn?" I gasped.

"Yeah, man, it's me. You okay?"

Unicorn and Jabberwocky helped me up to a sitting position. I blinked my eyes and shook my head, sending the discs of light off into the twilight.

"I'm okay," I said, finally, rubbing the back of my head.

"Sorry, dude, I didn't know anyone was there," Jabberwocky said.

"It's okay," I said slowly. "I'm fine."

"Christ, Jabberwocky, you are always in such a fuck of a hurry," Unicorn snapped.

"Hey, dude, you're the one who wanted that CD."

"That doesn't mean . . . forget it, forget it."

Jabberwocky shrugged his shoulders and bounded down the

sidewalk.

"What's going on?" I asked Unicorn as he helped me to my feet.

"Dave's back."

"Who?"

"My older brother Dave, back from Ireland."

"Penn?"

"That's right, man. And he went on that biking tour?"

I nodded, remembering.

"Well, he's back and havin' a bash for all his old prep school buddies."

Unicorn guided me through the front door into a blaze of light and music and punked-out teenagers, all dressed in black, hopping up and down. I slumped down on the bottom step of the staircase, still rubbing the back of my head.

The music was deafening.

"Stay right here," Unicorn commanded and disappeared into the jumping crowd.

He returned holding a plastic cup of something black.

"Drink this, man, you'll feel better," he shouted as he handed the cup to me.

"What is it?" I shouted back.

"Beer."

"Black beer?"

"It's a theme bash. All black."

"All black," I muttered as I looked into the cup at the foamy, gray head.

I studied Unicorn as I finished drinking the beer.

Black socks, black army boots unlaced. He had a studded dog

collar strapped around his neck and wore a black leather vest, open, without a shirt. Bermuda shorts, tie-dyed black. Kohl spattered around his clear gray eyes.

"Feeling better?" he asked.

"A little, but I've got to lie down for a minute."

"I'll walk you up."

At the top of the staircase on the third floor, I asked, "Is your mother here?"

"Huh?"

"Your mother."

"Nah, she went out to dinner with that new dipshit lawyer boyfriend of hers."

"But she knows about this party?"

"Of course she does."

I nodded.   Of course.

I opened the door to my room and flicked the light switch. A desk lamp turned on. I lay down on my bed.

"Do you want me to turn on the fan?"

"Thanks."

Unicorn pressed the button and the fan whirred, turning side to side. He sat down on the bed next to me.

"Better?"

"Much."

"That stupid Jabberwocky can't just walk or anything, he has to rush and dash and run all around."

"Well, it wasn't really his fault."

"He's still stupid anyway."

The sound of the fan filled the room and the floor vibrated with music.

"How's your friend?" Unicorn asked quietly.

I closed my eyes, suddenly seeing Matthew—his bald head, his gray skin, his white-encrusted lips.

"Not too good."

"I guess you want to be alone, huh?"

I nodded.

"Do you want another beer?"

"Not yet. Thanks, Unicorn."

Unicorn reached over, squeezed my thigh, and shook it. "I'm sorry 'bout your friend."

Tears slid behind my eyelids. I could only nod.

The bed rocked as Unicorn stood up. The door shut.

Matthew slammed into me then, knocking my breath out.

My mouth twisted open and for ten misshapen minutes, I cried, my voice snagged in my throat, my back hooked to the mattress, my hands embroidered on the comforter.

Tubes in his arms, his nose, his cock.

How could that have happened in a year? Turned into a shapeless mass of discolored flesh.

His breath lifting his chest with imperfection, lifting his chest with insignificance—the chest of a twenty-eight-year-old man. Deflating, disappearing.

A young man lost.

A vigorous young man lost.

A man I loved.

I sat up abruptly, grabbed a Kleenex from the side table, and wiped my eyes, blew my nose. I pulled off my shirt and threw it on the floor.

I stared at the Band-aid taped to the crook of my arm.

Had to have a blood test done. Routine. Dr. Thornton considered it imperative.

Did you have oral sex?Did you have anal intercourse?When was the last time?Who was passive?Who was active?

Talking about our sex life—our love—as if it were a machine or a car.

I sat rubbing my eyes, the back of my head throbbing from the smack against the sidewalk, my brain creaking with a headache.

I found Unicorn in the kitchen talking to one of the white girls who had skipped past me singing the Oz song. A boy with a tangerine crewcut was pouring himself a beer from the keg on the kitchen floor.

"Unicorn?"

"Hey, Zee, how's it going?"

"Do you have any aspirin?"

Without a word, Unicorn popped open the cabinet door next to him and pulled out a white-and-red plastic bottle. "Tylenol okay?"

"Tylenol is fine."

A girl with black, straight, shoulder-length hair thrust her head into the kitchen. "Hey, Margey, Ken's here."

"He is, is he?" Margey said indignantly and stomped out of the kitchen.

"Ken's gonna get it," Unicorn said, "Lucky for us the music is loud."

The boy with the tangerine crewcut followed her out of the room, carrying two cups of black beer.

"Do you want another beer, Zee?"

"Sure."

Unicorn poured me a beer.

Two boys, wearing dog collars and leashed to each other,

stumbled through the door.

"Grand Central Station," Unicorn said and smiled.

"Well, I'm going to take a stroll on Park Avenue," I said, opening the back door.

In the back yard, the heat dropped on me like a lost month.

A high wooden fence surrounded the long, narrow yard. Zinnias and dahlias bloomed orange and red and yellow along the edges of the fence. I sat down in a patio chair, waiting for the Tylenol to take hold. At the far end, near the picnic table, like a forgotten guest, sat a chestnut tree. The flickering flames of the torch lights tossed light into the branches of the tree. The tree was flowering, its tooth-edged leaves green and glossy, its catkins erect.

I gazed at the dark sky, found the Big Dipper and located Polaris, the North Star. Peary. The North Pole. The battles against the great white desolation.

I smelled it then—the odor of semen.

Surprised, I glanced around the yard, expecting to find a couple fucking in the zinnias.

I smelled it again—that unmistakable Chlorox odor. Semen. My memory ricocheted.

The chestnut tree.

I set my beer on the ground and walked to the tree. I pressed my face into its branches, inhaling. The catkins. In the humidity, the smell was moist and disturbingly erotic. I plucked a catkin from its branch and held it to my nose.

I remembered, as an adolescent, masturbating and holding the sticky spunk up to my nose, its sharp, unpleasant odor; remembered, as a teenager, sucking Ron's cock one night while camping out—how he ejaculated accidentally on my face and I smelled his semen, someone else's for the first time; remembered, during the

Summer of Sex, having anonymous sex with that black man in the park so many years ago.

I smelled the catkin again.

Remarkable, the similarity. How I had liked to watch Matthew come—my face close to his swollen cock, watching the hard head until the semen shot out in jerking sputters on his belly.

Eroticism, vitality, health.

Sex.

Sexual love.

Matthew. Wasting away in the turning world. Contaminated semen: spoiled—now the smell of death.

I shuddered and threw the catkin down to the ground.

I walked back to the patio chair, sat down, and drank my beer. I touched the Band-aid on the crook of my arm, then ripped it off—the pinprick dot.

I located the North Star again. The North Pole—an imaginary point in the great white desolation. Is that death? Is that the goal of our journey? The purity of ice and cold?

The back door opened and music pounded the night.

"Jabberwocky, you shouldn't drink any more beer."

"How come?"

"How come? Look at you."

Jabberwocky stumbled into the back yard. Unicorn followed him.

"Will you look at him?" Unicorn said to me.

Jabberwocky stood in front of me in his torn black tee shirt with WASHINGTON IS A CAPITOL CITY emblazoned on his chest in white. One of his spikes had wilted. He flopped down on the grass like a wounded walrus.

"Jesus," Unicorn muttered as he sat down next to me.

Jabberwocky smiled hideously, his eyes floating, said

slurringly, "Too much beer," leaned back, closed his eyes, and passed out.

"Jabberwocky?"

One of his legs slid down.

"Why do you call him Jabberwocky?"

"After that big fat slob in the *Return of the Jedi* flick. Y'know, the one who catches Princess Lea. What a dumb fuck he is. Doesn't know when to stop."

"Too much beer?"

"Yeah. Drinks too much and passes out. All the time."

"How old is he?"

"Fifteen."

"Fifteen and drinking beer?"

"The kids start early today."

"You don't drink, though, do you?"

"No way. You know that car accident my dad died in?"

I nodded.

"Drunk driver. That's why I'm not gonna drink. Ever."

Jabberwocky's other leg slid down and he let out a deep snore.

"He does this every time we go out and party."

"Why do you let him drink then?"

"I can't make him *not* drink."

"But you could discourage him."

"I s'pose. It's starting to be a bore. He passes out and I have to shake him and shake him to wake him up and then he just starts punching like a maniac and he's a strong kid, used to be on the football team his freshman year. Then I have to drag his ass back to his house or to my house to crash. Shit, I wish he had gone up to my room. You dumb fuck, Jabberwocky!"

"Well, you look out for him at least."

"If I don't, who will?" Unicorn said simply.

I could only shrug my shoulders in response.

If I don't, who will? Someone to look after you. A beginning point for love.

Jabberwocky farted.

"You dumb fat jerk," Unicorn said, laughing. "He'll fart all night long."

Miss Doin reassured me that she did not expect me to work through the summer while Dr. Ender completed his research.

If I don't, who will? Matthew and I should have made that our motto when we became lovers.

That night Glen called and asked if I wanted to go to Tracks, this terrific new nightclub in the Southwest. I hesitated.

As long as I instructed him on research methods and familiarized him with the Peary Papers, then she could manage to help him after that. I had three more boxes to examine and planned to complete them by June.

What do you know about love?

What do you say to a young man dying?

"Oh, come on, Zee, you haven't been out for a long time. It's Thursday night, the best night to go. The men are unbelievable."

"Okay, okay, what time?"

"I'll drop by at eleven-thirty. See you then."

The nightclub was immense, jammed with men.

Slippery eyes. Music shook the walls.

Over the dance floor lights flashed and glowed and twitched. After fifteen minutes, Glen disappeared into the dancing throng and left me alone.

I pushed my way through the crowd to the open-air deck for some relief from the smoke and the drumming music. I stood there only a short while when I noticed this man, slender and pale, with close-set eyes, glancing over at me. I flipped through my memory file trying to locate him, but I couldn't.   Finally, he walked over to me.

"Zee?"

"Yes," I said, "but I'm afraid—"

"Jerry," he said. "From Bootsie, Winkie and Miss Maud's?"

I nodded. Of course. The man with the eleven-inch cock and the malicious tongue. He works—or used to work—for the same escort service that Matthew had worked for. We almost always saw him when we had dinner at that restaurant.

"Well, how are you?" I asked.

"Can't complain. I'm still working at the restaurant, but I'm not with the escort service anymore. I have a lover now."

"That's great."

"I thought you moved out of town."

"I have. I mean . . . I did. I'm here just for a few months working on a special project at the National Archives."

"Have you seen Matthew?"

"No, I haven't."

"Does he know you're in town?"

"I doubt it."

Jerry looked at me perplexed.   "You mean he doesn't know you're here?"

"No. Matthew and I haven't been in touch since I left Washington."

"My God. You mean you don't know?"

"Don't know what?"

"Matthew's dying."

I felt the blood drain from my face and my eyes grow cold.

"He's in the hospital, Zee, at NIH. I thought you would have known."

Words stumbled in my throat.

Jerry seemed distressed and confused. "I'm sorry, I didn't—"

"Thank you. Thanks. If you'll excuse me."

I left Tracks.

After Mr. Wilson, the lawyer for the Peary family, left my office, Miss Doin expressed her displeasure at my incurious, distant attitude during the meeting.

What do you say

I walked from the Southwest

Underscoring the value and the importance of this acquisition,

to Capitol Hill

she advised me to draw up a proposal to submit to Mr. Wilson as soon as possible.

to downtown Washington

My mind, however, still raced with colors and shapes, patterns and balance.

to Dupont Circle

Riding home on the Metro, I could not look hard enough or long enough at the colors of clothes, the shapes of bodies, the linear perspectives of standing commuters.

to S Street

I stopped at a stationery store in Georgetown and bought colored paper, glue, pens, and a large pad of drawing paper.

to the Mckinnon townhouse.

I fixed myself a cup of coffee, sat down at the dining room

table, and started to cut and glue and draw.

My hands pulled my eyes over the surfaces.

My eyes pulled my mind over fields of imagination.

                                        The door clicked.

Matthew set his hands on my shoulders. "What's all this?"

"Doodling."

"Doodling? Looks a bit more involved than that."

I studied the sheet of paper in front of me, the strips of green paper pasted up along one side. Then I noticed the pair of scissors, the tip of the blades lying on the green stripes, the handles on the table top.

I stood up abruptly.

"Zee, what's up?"

I stared at the scissors and the green lines and then at the entire table top, littered with scraps of colored paper and a pile of drawings in one corner and the bottle of glue in the center.

I stood up on the chair.

"Zee, what the hell are you doing?"

        I stared down at the entire table top.

        The table top itself became . . .

                the patterns of the scissors and the colored scraps of paper became . . .

        I couldn't find the word,

                        couldn't form it.

"Matthew, look at the table top."

"Okay."

"What do you see?"

"Is this some kind of game?"

"No, no, what is it you see?"

Matthew looked baffled. "I see a pair of scissors and scraps of paper—"

"No. The whole thing. Everything together."

"I don't know what you're getting at?"

"There's a name for it."

"What do you mean? A name for all those collages you made?"

Collage.

"Let's see," he continued. "Collage collection, collage group, something like that?"

Collage. My doodlings were collage. The table top, in its random way, seemed like one huge collage.

"I didn't know you had an artistic bent," he said, looking up at me.

"Neither did I."

I turned one of the back rooms into a studio.

I bought supplies: an easel, paints, brushes, paper, canvases, pencils, paste, ribbon, cloth, and burlap.

All that summer and that fall of 1984, I devoted my evenings and my weekends to collage—the approach, initially, was that of a hobby.

On weekends, I was in the museums: The National Gallery of Art (East and West Wings), The Corcoran, The Hirschhorn, The Freer, The Phillips Collection.

I took day trips to The Baltimore Museum of Art, The Barnes Foundation, The Philadelphia Museum of Art, The Museum of Modern Art, and The Metropolitan.

A whole new world had opened for me—visual delectation.

I can't describe the excitement of the day trip I took to The Museum of Modern Art to see *Still Life with Chair Caning* (1912) by Picasso—the first collage. Four hours on the Amtrak in the morning, four hours in the museum that afternoon, and four hours on the Amtrak at night—an exhilarating, exhausting, stimulating day.

Since I spent so much time in museums and in the back room working on collages, I spent less and less time with Matthew and became less and less involved with my work at the National Archives. Miss Doin, in fact, had a discussion with me about my unfocused attention during the work day.

Time is lost to be gained.

By the spring of 1985, I had reached an impasse and fell into a Gauguin mood.

On the morning of April 23, 1909, when Peary reached the igloo at Cape Columbia, he wrote in his diary: "I have won the last great geographical prize, the North Pole, for the credit of the United States. This work is the finish, the cap and climax of nearly four hundred years of effort, loss of life, expenditures of fortunes by the civilized nations of the world, and it has been accomplished in a way that is thoroughly American. I am content."

One day, while working on a collage, it suddenly didn't matter to me if I ever saw Matthew again or if I ever walked into the National Archives again—time stealers.

Thoroughly American.

The next day at work, I was distracted, preoccupied, and distraught as I opened the final box of the Peary material. Inside I found in a protective wallet what looked like a small diary, no larger than four inches by seven. On the cover, in Peary's handwriting, which at this point I knew quite well, he had written: "No. 1, Roosevelt to ____& Return, Feb. 22 to Apr. 27, 1909, R. E. Peary, U.S.N."

I read the first page. This is the handwritten log of his North

Pole journey. I could scarcely believe I held this in my hand. I turned the pages to that historic date of April 6, 1909, but discovered that the page was blank—instead, a loose leaf page had been inserted with those historic words: "The pole at last!!! The prize of 3 centuries, my dreams & ambition for 23 years. <u>Mine</u> at last. I cannot bring myself to realize it. It all seems so simple & commonplace." How strange that those words had been written on a loose leaf page instead of in the actual diary. The pages for April 7th and 8th were also blank.

Dr. Ender knocked on my door.

"Dr. Ender," I said, standing up, "I found something you might find interesting."

"Yes?"

"Peary's North Pole log."

His eyes flashed and he did not move. I walked around my desk and held the small diary out to him. He looked at it, then up at my face, then down again to the small brown notebook in my hand. I could tell that he was reading the inscription on the cover. He exhaled deeply.

"I cannot believe this," he finally said. "This is the most important document in the history of all polar travel."

I handed the notebook to him. He took it with such slow movements and held it in his hands with such reverence that I thought of a priest's movements at the moment of transubstantiation.

"You cannot imagine what this means to me," he said. "Thank you, Zee. Thank you thank you." He turned and left my office, obviously having forgotten why he had knocked on my door in the first place.

I went back to the box and thought about what other treasures I would find. I shifted some of the papers around until I noticed a bundle of letters tied together with a red ribbon. I had never seen ribbon before in any of the boxes.

I read the top letter: Mrs. Mary Peary, 1632 19th Street, Washington, D.C.

My eyes twitched and my hands grew cold.

Peary's wife. Peary's love letters. The letters from his expeditions.

I placed my briefcase on the desk, opened it, and placed the letters inside.

What do you know about love?

When I shut the case, my heart clicked and my mind surged with a collage—the first time my imagination stirred since I had completed *Love Letters of Grandfather.*

What do you say to a young man dying?

When I left the building that night, I was sure the guard would stop me to inspect my briefcase, though he never had before. I gripped the handle, smiled, and walked past him outside to the sidewalk.

On the Metro, I didn't get off at the Dupont Circle stop, because I was going to see Matthew again, hoping that he would be awake this time, alert, aware of my presence.

Peary called the ice his treacherous antagonist.

The nurse led me into the room again.

Matthew was awake, awake but tired—his eyes dulled with exhaustion.

"Matthew?" the nurse said.

He moved his eyes.

"There's someone here to see you."

"Oh. Who is that?" he said hoarsely.

"Matthew?"

I moved to the side of the hospital bed as he turned his head slightly toward me.

"Matthew, it's Zee."

"Who?"

"Zee, Matthew, Zee."   I touched his hand, held his thin fingers.

I started to cry.

"It's Zee, Matthew."

He peered at me until recognition avalanched in his dark eyes."Oh, *Zee*."

He gripped my hand. "Zee, you."

Tears filled his eyes.

"Matthew, what happened? How could this have happened? To you? Why to you? Why couldn't this just be a bicycle accident?"

I bent forward, placing my forehead on his chest and sobbed.

All that energy of Van Gogh colors bounding up the stairs, asking, "You're not Zee, are you?"

That strong, solid body and that strong, solid face.

Gone.

How could that be gone? How?

Sitting in the chair by the window—this dashingly good-looking man, Mark.

This hustler, Mark. My Matthew. This man I love.

I stopped crying.

I breathed through my mouth and held the side of my face against his chest, listening to his heartbeat, distant and faint— grinding, groaning, creaking.

He coughed. I stood erect and gazed at him.

He gazed at me, his eyes like July.

The nurse handed me some Kleenex.

"Here, please sit down," and she moved a chair next to me as I blew my nose. "I'll be outside at the station if you need anything."

"Thank you," I said and sat down, "very much. I'm . . . I'm sorr—"

My face shifted.

She looked at me with a firm expression. "He's been waiting to see you all day." She had been crying too. She closed the door so that a wedge of fluorescent light shellacked the linoleum floor.

What do you say to a young man dying?

Matthew was twenty-eight years old.

Twenty-eight years old and dying.

I stared at the wedge of light, which disappeared when the clouds passed and let sunlight into the room.   The year was moving toward its longest day.

          The window was behind me so that as the wedge of fluorescent light disappeared, my shadow would form sketchily on the floor.

The clouds returned, the wedge of light reappeared, and my shadow vanished.

The window faces west then.

I sat sagged in this chair, watching the light come and go and my shadow form and unform.

I sat in the same position my grandfather had sat in when I saw him sitting next to my grandmother. I wondered if he had studied the shadow and the light on the floor.

I felt his eyes on me.

I turned to him—to this shadow of Matthew.

Oh, his jaw, his mouth, his eyes.

I repeated the name Matthew to myself as I peered into his cadaverous face.

He had lost most of his thick hair.

His pale purple eyelids hovered halfway over his eyes

     and his strong jaw jutted out like a jagged piece of ice.

          The corners of his mouth were caked with chalkiness.

His gray face, elongated through dramatic weight loss, resembled the faces in an El Greco painting.

The white sheets—it was as if he were lying in snow.

What do you say to a young man dying?

He indicated that he wanted water, so I placed the bent straw between his dry lips.

He sipped.

"That nurse is very nice," he said slowly.

I nodded.

"Do you know what her name is?"

I shook my head.

He smiled slightly. "Sabrina."

"No."

He nodded once and chuckled. "I was feverish when I came here and the doctor said that Sabrina would be taking care of me. I told him, 'But she can't do anything but sing.'"

We both laughed.

"Lovely Sabrina," I said.

"She's done quite well for herself, storming New York City. The critics don't know what to do with her since she's not impersonating singers or Hollywood film stars. A man who sings as a woman. That's the best they could do. Do you know she's releasing a CD this fall?"

"I didn't know. That's wonderful."

"Just think what would happen if one of her singles hits the Top Forty. What will Casey Cassum do? On the black charts we have . . . on the country and western charts we have . . . on the drag queen charts we have. . . ."

We both laughed again.

"When was the last time you saw Sabrina?" he asked.

"Oh . . . I guess about two or three years ago. That one time I Amtraked to New York to see the Manet show at the Metropolitan. I watched her show at the Tripoli, and we had drinks later on."

"Did you know she's in town?"

"Is she?"

"For about a week. She did a show here Friday. She's been traveling around the country doing benefit shows in hospitals for people with AIDS. In fact, part of the money she makes on her CD goes into AIDS educational programs in New York."

"Really," I said quietly.

"She's become the regular Florence Nightingale. She didn't know I was sick. After her show, when she came around to talk to us, she didn't recognize me until I told her who I was. I guess I'm unrecognizable now, huh?"

I nodded.

He looked away from me and peered abstractedly into space. "It is a terrifying disease. Do you remember how you said to me, the second night we were together, that I had winter in my eyes and summer in my blood?"

I nodded again.

"Well, now I have winter in my blood and summer in my eyes."

What do you say

"Anyway," he said, "she's staying at the Washington Hilton, and she'd love to see you. She asked about you, but I thought you were still in Maine, shut off from everything and everyone."

"Well, I had been. Making collages."

"I know. And you had a successful show last fall."

"How did you know?"

"I have my ways. You're making it work, aren't you?"

I smiled. "I am. I am making it work. And I'm talented, Matthew. I've got it."

"I always knew you had. You just had to find your means."

I told him about my year in Maine, the work I had accomplished, and the sense of happiness I had working with large canvases. I told him about the love-letters series, the explosion with my father over my grandfather's love letters, and how I was torn from the creative cycle and couldn't work. I told him I came down here for a change and ended up working again at the National Archives on this Peary project. And just today, the surge, the desire, the compulsion to work renewed itself when I discovered the Peary letters. I could tell I had strained his attention, and discomfort all of a sudden settled on my shoulders as I talked about my work and plans for a new collage and my wanting to return to Maine to work on it. I fell silent.

After a moment, he asked, "Where are you staying?"

"In Dupont Circle, on S Street, with the McKinnon family. I'll write down the telephone number and the address."

He asked for more water, and I placed the straw in his mouth again. I wiped the chalky substance from the corners of his mouth.

He stared at the ceiling, his manner distant and his face a struggle of expression.

"Zee?"

"Yes?"

"Why did you leave me?"

The question broke apart inside me.

"Why did I leave you?"

He stared at the ceiling. "I want to know."

Without hesitation, I said, "Oh, Matthew, everything. Everything seemed such a burden. The relationship, the city, the Archives, my father's carping about job security. Just everything. I couldn't separate one thing from another. It all just formed a huge rectangle of burden when all I wanted to do was to have the time to make collages."

I explained the sensation I had sitting in front of the Rothko.

"So you left just because you wanted to make art?"

"Yes."

He turned to me. "Did you ever stop loving me?"

I stared at his summer eyes.

Did I ever stop loving him?

"No," I said, jolted by the insight. I never had stopped loving him—the impulse to make collages had simply overpowered it. I had just gone away for a while, as though on a retreat, to pursue this other—this artwork. Have I ever been this obtuse? I never *had* stopped loving him.

"I never stopped loving you," I said in a hollow voice. "I just wanted . . . my God, Matthew."

"You just wanted to make collages."

I simply nodded.

Peary learned an obvious lesson in reaching the North Pole.

"Zee, would you do something for me?"

"Of course."

He considered it so obvious that he did not think it necessary to point it out to others, but he did.

"Would you lie next to me?"

"Here?"

"There's room."

I gazed into his face.

After 23 years of trial and error in Arctic exploration, his final plan, so carefully executed with such fidelity to detail, was comprised of numerous elements—the *absence* of any single one of them which would have been fatal to his success.

I lowered the bars and climbed into bed next to him.

"Hold me, Zee," he whispered. "Tight."

And I held him.

Tight.

This shadow of a man, this relic of a man, this memory of a man.

He fell into dreams in my arms.

What do you know about love?

After he fell asleep in my arms, I climbed out of bed and left the room.

I saw Sabrina, the nurse, look up from her desk at the station. She walked over to me.

"You made him very happy, Zee."

My face started to shift and crack again, but I held it firm.

I finished sifting through the contents of that last box—nothing as important as Peary's North Pole log, just miscellaneous letters to the Peary Arctic Club and some magazine articles he had saved.

"How long can he go on like this?"

The previous day crowded my mind and jumbled my thoughts.

"Most doctors are surprised he's gone on like this *this* long."

"I see."

This abrupt insight about my love for Matthew.

I held the briefcase tight in my hand.

I had not been with anyone else or even *desired* being with anyone else since I had left Washington. I wanted only to make collages.

No ache of separation, since I had not been separated.

I had only isolated myself to destroy myself to make collages.

I love Matthew.

Love Letters of Peary.

The collage twirled

through my mind as well as the taking

of the Peary love letters.

The stealing.

Is it stealing?

Should I return them?

No one would know they were taken.

But how would I explain the letters once I made the collage?

That they turned up in my mother's shop?

Or, since I discard material I don't think *relevant* for archival preservation, that rather than throw them away, I simply used them to make a collage?

Just talk to Miss Doin about taking them?

Make the collage and donate it to the National Archives?

This young man decomposing.

This young man I love breaking apart, falling apart like this old magazine article.

Dr. Ender knocked at my door.

Deeply preoccupied, he stepped into my office—hair uncombed, shirt wrinkled, eyes bloodshot—and walked straight to the bulletin board where I had the black-and-white photograph of Peary tacked up in one corner. He peered at the defiant visage. Thoughtfully, he rubbed his chin, then ran his fingers through his hair.

"I've been up all night," he said, still peering at the photograph, "studying maps, making computations, thinking and thinking about that log you found. That journal. That journal was the key, the final move on this maddening chess game of research. Look at that photo, Zee, and tell me what you see."

I looked at Peary's face. "Disappointment."

"Exactly!" he shouted. "That's why I thought it was a photo of Peary after the failed 1906 expedition, the same as you. That is not fatigue etched in his face."

"What do you mean?"

Dr. Ender turned to me. "Peary did not reach the North Pole."

I stared at him. "Are you sure?"

Dr. Ender rubbed both his hands over his exhausted, agitated face, then sat down in a chair. "No, I'm not abso*lute*ly positive. No one could be. But the evidence, especially that journal, points conclusively to failure. A limited failure, mind you, but still failure. According to my calculations, Peary was off the mark thirty to sixty miles. Let's go to my office, and I'll show you."

Dr. Ender sipped a cup of coffee as we studied a large map of the entire Arctic region spread out on a table.

Lines and circles of different colors were drawn on it to indicate Peary's route to the pole and Ender's calculations.

Dr. Ender spoke in terms of longitude readings, magnetic variations of compasses, sun readings, and drifting ice which I could hardly follow in his sleepless zeal of explanation. As far as I could understand, the ice fields drifted to the west which Peary did not account for with movements to the east to cancel it out. This carried him off his proposed route along the Cape Columbia meridian.

"But the most curious evidence is in that expedition journal you found, Zee. You looked at it, didn't you?"

I nodded.

"And did anything strike you as odd?"

"April 6th."

"Exactly, exactly. That fateful day and the pages were blank and a loose-leaf paper inserted with those famous words 'Mine at last!!!' written on it. An inserted page! April 7th was blank. April 8th. What must have gone through that man's mind when he took those crucial sun shot readings at midnight to discover he was not at the North Pole?"

Dr. Ender stared at the map.

With the dogs, the men, the experience, and the fixed determination that Peary likened to the same determination that drove Columbus over the trackless western sea, he knew that Destiny would favor a man who followed his faith and his dream ceaselessly to his last breath.

"Seventy-five years have gone by," he continued. "Is it possible that the greatest of polar explorers perpetrated a hoax upon the world? That his pride was so great? That he, perhaps, *refused* to believe failure? What am I supposed to do now, seventy-five years later?"

I called Sabrina. She was dashing out for an AIDS Charity Benefit at the Kennedy Center, but said to come over at midnight.

"Tell the truth."

Dr. Ender regarded me for a moment and whispered, "What is the penalty for destroying an American myth?"

At midnight I sat in the garish lobby of the Washington Hilton, my mind cramped with a medley of thoughts about Matthew, AIDS, Peary's love letters, and the collage—this clash of intense sadness and creative energy.

"But for all intents and purposes, even if Peary did not *literally* reach the North Pole, he did so

The lobby doors slid open and in strode Sabrina, still flamboyant, still beautiful.

virtually."

She strode straight over to me as I rose to greet her.

We didn't say a word.

We hugged each other and, holding each other, started to cry.

In her room she made me a gin and tonic.

"I hardly recognized him," I said.

"It's body rot, Zee, total body rot. It's merciless. I couldn't begin to tell you how many young men I've seen, wasting away, rotting like discarded fruit, shunned and despised. And the government, those fucking Republicans, has taken its sweet time about releasing funds. It's a disgrace, a simple disgrace in the face of humanity."

"I don't know what to do for him."

"You're doing what you can do, darling. Being with him.

That's the most important thing you can do for him right now. Just be with him."

I nodded and sipped my drink.

"How did you find out?" she asked.

"Someone told me in Tracks. He thought I knew."

She clucked her tongue. "Why didn't you keep in touch with him?"

I shook my head. "I don't know. I was busy with my fucking collages and wanted to be left alone. I didn't think—" I stared to cry again. "I didn't think something like this would have happened."

8,400 men had died of AIDS by June 1986.

She came to me and held me. "It's okay, Zee, okay."

"We talked about it. He understood. He—"

Miss Doin received a brown-paper-wrapped package marked Special Delivery.

"It's okay, darling, okay. You still love him, don't you?"

"My God, Sabrina, yes, I do."

"Does he know that?"

"Yes."

"Then cry, Zee, cry. No one could have given him anything better than that."

What do you know about love?

"East, west, and north had disappeared for us. Only one direction remained and that was south. Every breeze which could possibly blow upon us, no matter from what point of the horizon, must be a south wind. Where we were, one day and one night constituted a year, a hundred such days and nights constituted a century. Had we stood in that spot during the six months of the Arctic winter night, we should have seen every star of the northern hemisphere circling the sky at the same distance from the horizon, with Polaris (the North Star) practically in the zenith."

At four o'clock in the afternoon on April 7, 1909, Peary left the North Pole.

At ten o'clock in the morning on June 17, 1986, Matthew Curtis died.

I didn't go to work at the National Archives the next day or any day after that.

I packed.

My suitcase was on the bed as I folded shirts, setting them inside. The packet of Peary's love letters was on the bureau. My imagination swirled with *Love Letters of Peary*, and I was determined to make it—and to make other collages, more collages.

Unicorn knocked on my door, holding a package, wrapped in brown paper, large enough to hold a soccer ball. "So you're really leaving, huh?"

I set another shirt in my suitcase. "Have to."

He nodded.

"What's the package?"

"Oh, it's for you," he said, suddenly remembering that he held it in his hands. "It came this morning."

Unicorn laid the package on the bed. I looked at my name, then at an address in Maryland I didn't recognize. "I wonder what this is?"

"It's not heavy at all," Unicorn added.

I ran my finger along a flap of brown paper, ripping it open.

I pulled the scotch tape apart and pulled open the top of the box.

Inside, I found letters,

      all bundled together with rubber bands.

I lifted one packet:

Mr. Zeljko Matejcic, 1315 30th Street, NW, Washington, DC 20007.

Matthew's distinct handwriting.

I lifted another packet:

Mr. Matthew Curtis, 1315 30th Street, NW, Washington, DC 20007.

My own handwriting.

I lifted out another packet:

RETURN TO SENDER

"What are they?" Unicorn asked.

"Love letters."

What do you say to a young man dying?

Ted Wojtasik is the chairman of the Creative Writing Department at St. Andrews College in Laurinburg, NC. His first novel, *No Strange Fire*, based upon Amish barn fires in Big Valley of Pennsylvania, received a gold-starred review and "Editors' Choice 1996" in *Booklist* as well as a 1997 Silver Angel Award from Excellence in Media.

Collage, his second novel, is an experimental work about a Yugoslavian-American artist.

He has published book reviews and short stories in various literary journals. His short story "Scars and Frost" won Honorable Mention in O. Henry Festival Stories 2000, a national competition sponsored by Greensboro College. He holds an M.F.A. in fiction writing from Columbia University and a Ph.D. in Twentieth-century American literature from the University of South Carolina.